DISCARD

TROUBLE TIMES TWO

Center Point
Large Print

Also by James J. Griffin and available from Center Point Large Print:

Ride for Justice, Ride for Revenge
Bullet for a Ranger
The Zombies of Zapata
The Ranger
To Avenge a Ranger
Murder Most Fowl - Texas Style
The Ghost Riders
Tough Month for a Ranger
Fight for Freedom
Renegade Ranger
Texas Jeopardy

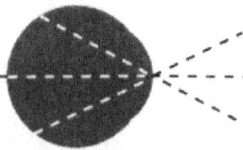

TROUBLE TIMES TWO

A Texas Ranger Luke Caldwell Story

James J. Griffin

CENTER POINT LARGE PRINT
THORNDIKE, MAINE

This Center Point Large Print edition
is published in the year 2022 by arrangement with
the author.

The text of this Large Print edition is unabridged.
In other aspects, this book may vary
from the original edition.
Printed in the United States of America
on permanent paper sourced using
environmentally responsible foresting methods.
Set in 16-point Times New Roman type.

ISBN: 978-1-63808-527-0

The Library of Congress has cataloged this record
under Library of Congress Control Number: 2022942408

1

Texas Ranger Lieutenant Luke Caldwell stood in a slight crouch. His hand hovered just over the butt of the Colt Peacemaker in the holster hanging at his right hip. Twenty feet away, two others, both fast guns, stood facing the Ranger. In the next few moments, either the Ranger or the gunslingers would lie dead.

The blazing afternoon Texas sun beat down on Luke. Circles of sweat stained the armpits of his light blue shirt. A rivulet of more perspiration trickled down his spine. He swallowed to force down the lump in his belly. No matter what some might claim, Luke felt fear every time he faced another man over loaded guns. Anyone who claimed they didn't was a liar, a fool, or both. They were also the men most likely to do something reckless, and end up dead.

Luke studied the two young gunfighters facing him. The one on the right had piercing, deep blue eyes, almost the same shade as Luke's. Their gaze seemed to bore clean through the Ranger as the gunman glared back at him, his expression one of grim determination. The gunman on the left had eyes of light brown. They were unreadable to Luke, as was this man's expression, until a slight smile played across his lips. He was clearly the more dangerous of the two. But, was he the more accurate with a six-gun? Once the shooting started, Luke would only have a split second to make that decision. Would it be easier for him, being right handed, to take out the man on the right first, then hope he could shift his aim quickly enough to get the second, before he felt the impact of hot lead ripping into him? Or should he try for the man on the left first, hoping his instincts were right, and the other man would be slower, giving Luke time to nail him before he could pull the trigger?

Seconds ticked by. Both gunmen grabbed for their weapons at the same moment. Luke yanked his Colt from its holster. The blue-eyed gunman was just bringing his revolver level when Luke shot him in the chest. Knowing the man was probably dead, but definitely out of the fight, Luke didn't wait to see him spin and fall. He realized he was too late as he shifted his gun to the brown-eyed gunslinger. That one already had his gun out, and aimed directly at Luke's gun belt's buckle. He lifted the barrel of his gun just a fraction, thumbing back the hammer. He pulled the trigger, and shot Luke in the belly. Luke clutched his middle with his left hand and staggered. He managed to hang onto his gun, and with the last of his strength put a return shot into the brown-eyed gunman's stomach. The young man screeched, dropped his gun, and clamped both hands to his belly. He jackknifed, crumpled to his knees, fell onto his side, and rolled onto his back. Luke, his life ebbing away, stumbled up to him and kicked his gun out of reach. He turned to check on the killer's partner, who was lying face down. With the toe of his boot, Luke rolled him onto his back. The man's body rolled loosely, his blue eyes were shut tight. He showed no signs of life.

"Is . . . muh brother . . . dead?" the brown-eyed gunman asked.

"He sure is," Luke answered. "I reckon you don't have long, neither."

"You . . . ya gut-shot me," the dying man said, fixing Luke with an accusing stare. "Worst way . . . for a man . . . to die."

"Only did . . . same thing you did . . . to me. Ya plugged me plumb in the middle . . . of muh . . . belly," Luke answered. "Least you won't be . . . doin' . . . any more . . . killin'."

"Neither will you, Ranger. I took you with me'n . . . my brother."

Luke collapsed onto the stairs next to where the two gunslingers had fallen, with his bullets in them. He took his last breath a moment after the brown-eyed gunman shuddered and his body went slack.

The brown-eyed gunman struggled to his feet. He stood over Luke and glared at the downed Ranger.

"Pa, that wasn't fair," he complained. "Johnny wasn't ready. You plugged him before givin' him a chance to draw."

Luke, who was home on leave, opened his eyes and looked up at Donny, his seven-year-old son. The boys had pleaded with him to play a game of gunfighters.

"Your brother had his chance. I got him fair and square. It ain't my fault he's a mite slow on the draw. Besides, if you'd been quicker, you could have shot me again. Then I'd've been dead before I drilled you. And why're you complainin' about bein' gut-shot? You did the same to me."

Johnny, Luke's ten-year-old son, Donny's older brother, added his voice to the disagreement.

"Pa got us both, Donny. He done killed you just like he done killed me."

"He couldn't have," Donny protested. "I got him first, right smack in the belly. He was already dead, soon as I plugged him."

"Ah, but that's where you're wrong, Donny boy," Luke said. "You didn't make certain of that. You should've put two or three slugs into me, rather'n just one. *That* would've finished me off."

"I still say you were dead," Donny insisted.

"There's only one way to find out," Johnny said. "We're gonna have to fight again. That'll prove one way or the other who's faster."

"Uh-uh. I'm finished," Luke said. "I've got to get back to fixin' the barn door."

"You can't quit. Not until we know who's faster," Donny protested, just as a man on horseback rode up.

"The boy's right, Luke," Major John B. Jones, commander of the Frontier Battalion, said, with a laugh. The major's thick, drooping moustache was as dark as sorghum. He gazed steadily at Luke from where he sat, atop his sturdy bay gelding.

Luke scrambled to his feet. He sketched a hasty salute.

"Major Jones. Howdy, Sir. I wasn't expectin' you until tomorrow."

"I got an early start, and you don't need to salute me, Luke. You know that. The Rangers aren't the United States Army."

"Boys, say howdy to Major Jones," Luke ordered. "Major, you remember my sons, John and Donald."

Both Luke's boys murmured their greetings.

"Howdy, boys. I certainly do remember you," Jones answered. "You've both grown quite a bit since the last time I saw you. How about your girls, Luke?"

"Deborah and Molly? They're growin' like weeds too," Luke answered. "They've gone into town, to do some shopping with Adeline. They should be back in about an hour. Why don't you get down and make yourself comfortable until they return? The boys can put up your horse."

"We can't, Pa," Donny protested. "We haven't finished our gunfight yet."

"Just do what I asked. Me'n Major Jones need to talk in private," Luke answered.

"No, the boy's still right, Luke," Jones said, grinning. "Unless you're too lily livered to face these two young'ns again. If you are, that means you're washed up as a Ranger."

"You're serious, Major?"

"Da . . . I mean, dang right I am. I also want to see how fast these two really are. If they can beat you to the draw, there's a spot waiting for them in the Rangers, soon as they're old enough."

"Do you really mean that, Major Jones?" Johnny asked.

"I don't say anything I don't mean."

"You hear that, Pa?" Donny said. "So are ya gonna fight us again, or do ya have a yella streak up your back?"

"I'm not afraid of you two," Luke snapped. "Let's get this over with."

Donny and Johnny shoved the non-working Smith and Wesson American revolvers they held back into their pants' waistbands. Luke picked up the non-functioning old Colt Navy he was using and slid it back into his holster. The firing pins had been removed from all three guns. Even if the guns had been loaded, there was no chance of one being accidentally fired.

Once again, Luke and his boys went into their gunfighter's stances.

"Go for your gun, ya no good, yella-bellied sidewinder," Johnny yelled.

Luke grabbed for his six-gun. He hadn't even cleared leather before both boys aimed and fired. Luke grunted, and dropped his gun. He grabbed at his belly. Before he finished falling, the boys each shot twice more. Luke pitched to his face.

"We got him!" Johnny triumphantly shouted.

"We'd best make sure he's dead," Donny answered.

They walked up to the downed Ranger and rolled him onto his back. Luke lay unmoving.

"Looks like we plugged him right in the heart," Johnny said. "He didn't have a chance."

"And the guts," Donny added. "We got him good. He's done for. That's for certain. We didn't miss one shot."

"Good work, boys," Jones said. "That's one renegade who'll never bother honest folks in Texas again."

"So does that mean we get to be Texas Rangers?" Johnny asked.

"It certainly does, soon as you're old enough."

Luke spoke up from where he lay on the ground.

"And I guess I just lost my Ranger commission."

"You're not getting off that easy, Luke. As soon as you pick yourself up, we'll talk."

Luke stood up. He beat the dust from his pants and shirt.

"No point in keepin' you waitin', Major. Boys, you take care of the major's horse. Feed him and brush him down, good. Take care of Pete and RePete while you're at it."

"All right, Pa."

Jones dismounted, and handed Johnny his horse's reins. They led the horse around to the stable out back. Luke led Major Jones through the office of the Junction *Clarion* newspaper, which his wife owned and published. They went to the living area behind the office, and headed into the kitchen.

Luke poured two mugs full of thick, black coffee from the pot simmering on the stove. He handed one to Major Jones. Both men sat at the kitchen table. Luke rolled and lit a cigarette, while Jones took a pouch of tobacco and his pipe from his jacket pocket. He filled the pipe, lit it, and took a long puff before speaking.

"Luke, I'm certain you've figured out by now that I've got to cancel the remainder of your leave," he said. "I've decided to make a few changes in the way the Frontier Battalion operates. We're looking at a real bad situation in far West Texas. I need you to leave for there right away."

"That's not a problem, Major," Luke answered. "Addie and the kids will be a bit disappointed, but they'll understand. Plus, much as I hate to admit it, at least to them, I'm ready to get back to work. That's just between you and me, of course."

"I understand, Luke. Most of the men under my command are itchy footed. It's the reason many of them joined the Rangers in the first place. How soon will you be ready to travel?"

"Tomorrow, if need be."

"I'd be obliged."

"Then I'll leave right after sunup," Luke answered. "Exactly where am I headed for? Where will I meet up with my company?"

"Presidio County. But you won't be meeting up with your company. That's part of the change in tactics I just mentioned. You're going in alone."

"Alone?"

"That's correct. Yes, usually I send in an entire company of Rangers to clean out the renegades from an area. However, as you know, sometimes all that does is drive the men we're after out. They move on before we can round up most of them. That's one reason I'm sending you on this assignment solo. The other is, from the information I've gathered, you won't be going up against several outlaw bands. It appears, except for the always present loners, or pairs, you'll be searching for one particular outfit. That's the other reason I'd like to keep your presence in Presidio unknown for as long as possible. However, once the men you'll be searching for are aware of your presence, they most likely won't be frightened off by just one man, even a Ranger."

"No, they won't. They'd rather shoot me in the back from ambush and be done with it."

Luke gave a rueful smile.

"You always did cut to the chase, Luke," Jones said. "Of course, if you'd rather turn down this assignment . . ."

"Not a chance."

"I knew that would be your answer. I've got a file in my saddlebags I'll give you. You can study that on your way. However, I'll provide you the basic information you need, now. You'll be trying to track down a gang of about half a dozen men, mebbe two or three more, or less. They seem to be conducting most of their raids along the borders of Presidio County. You know the state has been talking about carving some new counties out of Presidio, which right now covers an awful lot of territory. It's far too much area for the Presidio County sheriff and his men to cover. The county sheriff's name is Wilbur Clayton. I don't know much about him, so you'll have to judge him for yourself once you meet him. I'm certain that's one reason the men we're after are working where they are. It's mighty rugged country. Real easy for them to make a raid, then escape by fading into the tall and uncut. By the time word gets back to the sheriff's office in Marfa, they've long since disappeared. Your job is to make certain they don't."

"Should be simple enough."

"Don't make light of the situation, Luke. You're one of the few men I would ask to take on this task, single-handed. And of course there'll probably be other outlaws you'll come across."

"I appreciate your confidence in me, Major. It's about three hundred miles from here to Marfa. Leavin' tomorrow should get me there in a week to ten days."

"Take the ten days if you need to. I'd rather you didn't wear yourself, and your horses, out before you even get to your destination."

"That's good advice, Major. I'll take it."

"Good. Now, let let's go over what we can before your wife and daughters get back. Also before your boys finish caring for the horses. There's no need to worry them more'n necessary."

"You know Addie will insist on you staying for supper, and spending the night," Luke said.

"I know she will. I'm looking forward to some of her good cooking."

"She'll most likely want to put a story about

your visit in her newspaper. Probably will even want to have your photograph taken, too. We've got a photography shop in town now."

"I won't object to that. As long as she doesn't print any information that might be helpful to the outlaws in these parts. So many of them always seem to be one step ahead of us."

"Addie's extremely discreet about what she prints. You can count on that, Major."

"Excellent. Now, I'll just pour myself another cup of coffee. Then we can get to work."

2

Luke and Major Jones left an hour after sunrise the next morning. They had wanted to leave at first light, but Adeline wouldn't hear of it. She insisted both men have breakfast with the family before departing, especially after hearing that Luke would most likely be gone for at least a month and a half, probably more. After one last, lingering kiss between Luke and his wife, and farewell hugs and kisses for his children, the two lawmen were finally on their way. They rode together to the west edge of town, where Jones would turn southwest, while Luke kept riding almost due west.

"I'm sorry again about the late start, Major, but when Addie gets her mind set, there's no changin' it."

Jones waved his hand at Luke.

"I've already told you, it's no problem. You'll be away from your family for quite some time. And of course there's always the possibility, however remote, that you might not return at all."

"With all due respect, I'm not certain how 'remote' that possibility is, Major," Luke answered. He grinned.

"Lieutenant, if I didn't believe you were the man for this job, I wouldn't have chosen you,"

Jones said. "I'm certain you'll get it done."

"Thanks, Major. Besides, it *is* nice leavin' on a full belly, especially since I don't know when I'll get a home-cooked meal again."

Jones leaned back in his saddle and patted his stomach.

"I can't disagree with you on that, Luke. Supper last night was also delicious. I also appreciate the extra trail rations she packed for us. Those'll keep us off bacon and beans for a couple of days. Your wife's a fine cook. How she keeps house, raises four kids, and runs a newspaper all at the same time, while you're mostly gone, traipsin' all over Texas chasing desperadoes, is a plumb mystery to me."

"She's a wonder all right," Luke agreed. "A real treasure. The day I met Addie was the best day of my life. The Lord truly blessed me when she agreed to be my wife. Honestly, it's the womenfolk like my Addie who will finally tame Texas. Us men sure haven't done much of a job at that."

"Boy howdy, you've sure got that right," Jones said. He laughed, then pulled his hat from his head to wipe sweat from his brow.

"Luke, I meant what I said about you not rushin' too hard on your way to Marfa. The heat's brutal already, and it's not yet eight o'clock in the morning. Temperatures like this can kill a man almost as easily as an outlaw's bullet,

18

or an Indian's arrow. Hard on the horses, too."

"I won't push Pete and RePete too hard," Luke answered. "Once I'm closer to Presidio County, I'll get off the main road, and cut cross country. I figure soon as I cross the Pecos I'll swing southwest, and head directly for Alpine. That'll keep me away from Fort Stockton. The fewer people who see me until I can get somewhat of a handle on the situation I'm up against, the better."

"That sounds like a right smart plan, Luke. Just be careful. Send a wire to me when you're able."

"Will do, Major. Adios."

"Vaya con Dios, Luke."

Luke watched Jones ride away, until the major was out of sight. He nudged his dull spurs into Pete's sides.

"C'mon, boy, get up there."

Luke rode steadily all day, stopping only to rest his horses, and shortly after noon to have a meager lunch of jerky and biscuits, washed down with tepid water from his canteen. He'd save the sandwiches Addie had made for supper. He was following, for now, the main road that ran from Austin through Junction, west to Fort Stockton, then on to El Paso. It crossed semi-arid high plains and desert. In the vicinity of Junction, the land was rolling, interspersed with occasional low hills. Vegetation was fairly thick, consisting of grasses, cactus, scrub brush, and dry climate tolerant trees, such as mesquite and scrub oak. Some junipers managed to survive in damper spots. Cottonwoods and a few cedars grew along the banks of the North Llano River. As he continued farther west, the terrain leveled out. The vegetation gradually thinned out, giving way to mostly desert shrubs and cactus.

The road, for this desolate section, was fairly busy, with solitary riders, groups of horsemen, and mule or ox driven freight wagons. Luke did little more than nod to the travelers he encountered. While the Texas and Pacific Railroad was building west across Texas, with eventual plans to reach San Diego, California, the railroad had chosen a more northerly route. Eventually the Texas and Pacific would abandon its intentions to build all the way to the West Coast, instead terminating at Sierra Blanca, Texas, where it met the tracks of the Southern Pacific. Here, farther south, public transportation still relied on stagecoaches. The C. Bain and Company Stage Line's main route ran from San Antonio to Fort Concho, but a regional route, which connected with the primary stage road farther west, followed the same road which Luke was traveling. With sunset less than an hour away, Luke decided to spend the night at the next stage relay station.

"We're almost done for the day, fellers," he told his tired horses. "You'll get good feed and water.

Enjoy it, because it might be the last you see for a while."

Pete tossed his head. Following alongside, RePete snorted.

"Any more smart remarks and neither one of you'll get fed at all tonight," Luke warned. "There's the station, just ahead. Get on up there. Rattle your hocks."

He put the geldings into a trot. Five minutes later, he rode through the gate in the high adobe wall which surrounded the relay station. Like most stage line facilities in the Southwest, the station had been designed as a fortification against raiders, be they Indians, Mexicans, or Whites. The gate in the thick wall was just wide enough for a stagecoach and team of horses to pass through. The station itself was also built with thick adobe walls. The windows were small and high up, to protect its occupants. The walls also kept the interior cooler in summer and warmer in winter. A parapet around the roof provided cover for riflemen, who would be stationed there in the event of an attack.

There was nothing about Luke's appearance to mark him as a Texas Ranger. He kept his badge in his vest pocket. His usual trail outfit of sweat-stained, light-colored Stetson, plain light blue shirt, brown roughout leather vest, faded denims, scuffed black boots, and a red silk bandanna looped around his neck was no different than that of any of a thousand other drifting cowhands or horse wranglers. Except for a second look at his rare twin paint horses, Luke was a man who ordinarily wouldn't rate much more than a glance, perhaps a nod, from most others. Yet there was something about the tall, lean Ranger, with his jet black hair and moustache, contrasted with his piercing blue eyes, that commanded men's, and women's, attention. After he'd married Adeline, Luke had learned to ignore, or fend off, the advances of the painted women who frequented saloons, dance halls, and brothels. As far as men, he could usually tell, without too much effort, whether their interest was just in meeting a passing stranger, determining if they were looking for trouble, or on the run from the law.

Three men were tossing hay to horses in the corral when Luke rode in. One of them, holding a rifle, turned to meet Luke. He met Luke's steady gaze with one of his own as he sized up the new arrival. One look told him that somehow, even though he had the drop on the rider, if shooting started, he'd be the one to eat lead.

"Evenin', stranger," he said. "What can I do for you?"

"The handle's Luke. Wonderin' if I could get a meal, and a bunk for the night? Stablin' for my horses, too."

"I reckon. Rate's a dollar for the bunk. Includes

supper and breakfast. Fifty cents to put your animals in the far corral, away from the stage horses and mules. They'll get half a bucket of oats, water, and all the hay they can handle."

"Sounds fair," Luke said.

"My boys'll help you get your horses settled. Todd! Matt!"

"Yeah, Pa?" one of the boys answered.

"This man's gonna be spendin' the night. Help him get his horses put up."

"All right, Pa."

Both boys, one about eighteen, the other around twelve, put down their pitchforks and shuffled across the dusty courtyard to join their father and Luke.

"My name's Wayne Hawkins," the relay station agent said, once the boys reached them. "These are two of my sons. Todd's the oldest one. Matt's the young'n of the family. I've got two more boys, Jamie and Hank. They're gettin' the team ready for the incoming stage. My wife, Louisa, is inside, cookin' supper, along with our daughters. It'll be ready in about an hour. There's a pump and trough out back where you can wash up."

"Appreciate that," Luke said.

"These are two good lookin' horses, Mister," Todd said. "Never seen two which look so much alike. They almost could be twins."

"That's because they are," Luke said, with a grin. "The one I'm ridin's Pete. His brother's

RePete. They were lucky. Hardly any twin foals survive. They got lucky again when I stumbled across their owner. He was gonna sell 'em for dog food. I could tell they were good horses, and he sold 'em to me, cheap."

"If you don't mind my askin', Luke, what brings you this way?" Wayne said. "You don't strike me as just another chuck line ridin' cowhand."

Luke chuckled.

"I've been that, and a lotta other things. Right now, I'm just passin' through. Headin' west, to see what I might turn up. I've always been fiddle-footed. Guess I always will be."

"All right. I reckon you don't want to tell me who you really are, or what you're up to. That's your privilege. I won't press you any further."

"You're one sharp hombre, Wayne."

"So I've been told, Luke. I'm gonna get back to work. My wife'll show you where to bunk. I'll see you at supper."

"A home cooked meal sure sounds good," Luke said. "Long as your boys don't mind, I'll rub down my horses myself. They're not happy unless I do. Plus, if I don't give 'em a piece of licorice or leftover biscuit, they won't be pleased. They'll make my life miserable tomorrow."

"Oh, you've got a couple of pie-biters here," Matt said. "Kind of spoiled, are they?"

"Or biscuit-eaters, take your pick," Luke

answered. "And they're not just kind of spoiled. They're spoiled rotten."

Pete put his nose in Luke's back, and shoved hard. RePete shook his head and nipped at Luke's sleeve.

"I see what you mean," Matt said, laughing. "We'd better get these two fed, before they get angry at us."

After caring for his horses and washing up, Luke headed inside the station. He was greeted by a slender Mexican woman, who was about the same age as her husband.

"Hola, Luke," she said. "I hope you don't mind me using your name."

"Not at all . . . Louisa," Luke said, giving her a reassuring smile.

"These are my ninas, Molly and Theresa."

"Pleased to meet all of you."

"The senors' bunk room is on the left, if you'd like to take a siesta before supper," Louisa said. "The eastbound stage is late, which is not unusual. I try to wait supper until it arrives. I hope you don't mind."

"Not at all," Luke answered. "I've had a long day in the saddle, so some rest before I eat sounds mighty fine. Whatever's cookin' sure smells good."

"I'm afraid it's nothing special. Rabbit stew, tortillas, and beans."

"Mi madre did make her cinnamon cookies today, though. They're really good," Theresa said.

"I'll bet they are," Luke said, with a smile. "The stew also sounds mucho bueno. Pretty much anythin' is better than the bacon and beans I make."

"I helped with the tortillas," Molly added.

"Then they must taste extra special, too."

"That's enough, ninas," Louisa said. "Mr. Luke needs some rest. Luke, you may take any of the cots you like. We'll wake you when the stage rolls in."

"I'm sure I'll hear it, but I appreciate that."

Luke went to the men's bunk room, where, always cautious, he chose the bunk in the back corner, from which he could see anyone else entering the room, but no one could get behind him. He tossed his saddlebags on the floor alongside the bed, placed his Winchester next to them, and hung his hat on the peg behind the bunk. He sat on the edge of the cot, removed his boots, but left his gun belt buckled around his waist, and stretched out on the thin, straw and corn husk filled mattress. In less than five minutes, he was sleeping soundly.

3

Luke was awakened by several gunshots, as well as the thundering of hooves and the rattling of the stagecoach, as it entered the station yard at high speed. It was now full dark. He jumped out of bed, pulled on his boots, picked up his rifle, and raced outside. The stage was just coming to a stop. Tied behind it were two horses, carrying bodies draped belly down over their saddles. The driver's left arm was supported by his neckerchief, turned into a makeshift sling. The left side of his shirt was blood soaked. When the horses halted, he slumped over in his seat and dropped the lines.

"What the hell happened?" Wayne shouted.

"Robbery," the shotgun guard answered. "They came out of the brush at us a few miles back. Got Charlie in his arm and side, but I blasted both of 'em before they could do any more harm. They'd cut down a bunch of mesquites, and had those blockin' the road, so it took a spell to clear the way enough to get through. Good thing there was just enough light left for us to see the damn barricade. If we'd run into it at full speed, there'd have been nothin' but the pieces left to pick up."

"Anyone else hurt?" Luke asked.

"The passengers got jounced around a lot, so

they'll be a bit sore," the guard answered. "And one lady fainted. She's fine."

"Enough talk, Maxwell Caulfield," Louisa said to the guard. "Help Charlie down from there so I can tend to his wounds. Molly, Theresa, take the passengers inside. Start feeding them. With the stage being so late, and the attempted robbery, they must be starved."

"I don't reckon you'll be pullin' out before daylight, Mack," Wayne said to the guard, as they took the driver from his perch.

"You reckon right," Caulfield answered. "Charlie won't be in any shape to drive, and the passengers need some time to settle down."

"Don't you tell me whether I can or can't drive a coach, damn it!" Charlie snapped. "I've pulled coaches through when I was in far worse shape'n this. Soon as Louisa patches me up, I'll be ready to roll."

"You'll let me be the judge of that, Charles Mayfield," Louisa answered. "Get inside so I can look at that arm, and your side."

"Yes'm," Charlie muttered.

"No one argues with Louisa, leastwise not if they know what's good for 'em," Wayne said to Luke. "Jamie, Hank, grab these here horses and take care of 'em. Make certain to rub 'em down good. Cool 'em off before you let them eat or drink. We can't have any animals founderin' or colickin'. Unhitch the other team and put 'em away, too. They ain't goin' anywhere tonight."

"Sure, Pa," Jamie answered. "C'mon, Hank."

"Matt, Todd, untie those horses from behind the coach. Give me a hand with those dead hombres. We'll put the bodies in the harness shed for tonight, then plant 'em out back come daylight."

"I'll do that, Wayne," Luke offered. "That way your boys can help their brothers with the teams."

"I'd be obliged. I'll come with you. Two pairs of hands'll make shorter work."

The horses carrying the bodies were untied, and led to the shed alongside the barn. The dead men were laid on the floor. They were young, one tow-headed, the other sandy haired. Both had gray eyes, which were still open. Their faces were frozen in an expression of shock and fear. Each had taken a full load of buckshot in the chest.

"These two hombres weren't much more than kids," Luke exclaimed. "I'd bet my hat neither one ain't even twenty years old. Looks like they could be related, mebbe cousins, or even brothers. Awful young to try robbin' a stage."

"They made a big mistake in takin' on a coach with Mack Caulfield ridin' shotgun," Wayne said. "He ain't never come out of a tangle with highwaymen on the losin' side yet. These boys might be older'n they look. Or mebbe they've been trouble since the day they were born."

29

"Could be," Luke said. "I'm gonna go through their pockets and saddlebags. See if they have any way of bein' identified. They might already have wanted dodgers out on 'em. Or perhaps there'll be somethin' so their next of kin can be notified."

"You can't," Wayne protested. "You ain't got the right."

Luke pulled his badge from his vest pocket.

"Actually, I do. Texas Ranger."

Wayne whistled.

"Well, I'll be damned. Knew you were more'n just a driftin' cowhand passin' through. Never figured you for a Ranger, though."

"Well, I *am* passin' through," Luke answered. "But now I've got to file a report on this attempted holdup. Let me see if these bodies can tell me anythin'."

"Dead men ain't gonna do any talkin', Ranger."

"Not exactly. But they still might speak."

Luke went through the dead men's pockets, finding nothing more than some coins and folding money, along with matches, sacks of Bull Durham, and cigarette papers. The contents of their saddlebags also yielded no clues.

"Nothin', huh, Luke?"

"Nope. They're guns aren't in their holsters. I reckon the guard just tossed those in the coach. I'd like to take a look at them."

"It's around back. Follow me."

Luke trailed Wayne behind the station. He took a lantern from its wall bracket, then climbed to the driver's seat. He shone the light on a fresh hole in the wall behind the perch.

"Only one bullet hole," he said. "That most likely means one of the slugs is still in your driver. Bullet must've gone through his arm, then into his side. Seems like whichever of those boys did the shootin' panicked, and pulled the trigger without thinkin'. Just started firin' his gun. Bad mistake. Of course, tryin' to rob a stage was a big mistake in the first place."

Luke climbed down, and opened the right door to the passenger compartment. Two six-guns were lying on the floor.

"These must've belonged to the dead men." He picked one up, spun the cylinder, then smelled the barrel.

"This one ain't been fired."

He repeated his actions with the second revolver.

"This one's been fired. Two bullets missin' from the chambers, and you can still smell the powder smoke."

He took a quick look around the cabin.

"There's the hole where the bullet came out, then another where it went through the roof. Probably buried in a piece of baggage. No point in lookin' for it. Not much more we can find out here. Let's head inside. I want to see how

31

the driver is doin', talk to him if I can. I'm also gonna question the guard and passengers. I'll need their statements for my report."

"Mebbe you can get those while we're eatin'. I'm plumb starved," Wayne said.

"They'll have to be in writing. Long as you have paper and pencil, I can get them down while we eat. Or I can bring some in from my saddlebags."

"There's no need," Wayne said. "I've got plenty."

"Bueno. Let's go."

Tired from the long day, even after his earlier rest, Luke wanted nothing more than to turn in and get some sleep, before starting out again in the morning. However, at Louisa's insistence, he had to wait until supper was finished before he could interview the guard and passengers from the stage. The driver had slipped into a coma, with a high fever, but Mrs. Hawkins had been able to locate and remove the bullet lodged in his side. She assured Luke that he would recover, with rest and care. As soon as Luke finished his questioning, he wrote up a report for Headquarters, which would go out in the morning mail, when the stage which had been held up continued its journey, driven by Mack Caulfield, the shotgun guard, in place of the driver. Once that was done, Luke went back to his bunk. He slept undisturbed by the snoring of his bunkmates, nor was he bothered by the lumpy, thin mattress. After an early breakfast, he resumed his westward journey.

4

By using two horses, Luke could make better time than a rider with a single mount. Alternating horses daily meant less work for each, leaving them with more stamina for crucial moments. Today, he was riding RePete, with Pete carry Luke's much lighter packsaddle.

The heat this day was even more intense than usual for mid-summer in Texas. Besides the sun beating down, making Luke feel like he was baking, the humidity was also high, with moisture drifting in from the Gulf of Mexico on a light southeasterly breeze, which provided no relief. On top of that, the Ranger was itching all over, suffering the bites of what felt like thousands of fleas, bedbugs, and lice. By noon, he'd reached the end of his rope.

"RePete, I dunno about you, but I'm done," he said to his horse. The paint tossed his head in seeming agreement. "I've slept in lots of places with fleas and bedbugs, but never one as infested as that relay station. We're gonna turn off the road. I'll find a spot where I can strip off my duds and take a bath. Mebbe you'n your brother'll want to take a dip, too. Get some of the trail dust off, and keep the horseflies away, at least for a spell. We'll rest until dark, mebbe a bit longer.

Then, we'll travel the remainder of the night, and hole up durin' daylight again tomorrow, if it's still this damn hot. Now I know why they say the Devil takes his vacations in Texas."

The road Luke was traveling roughly paralleled the course of the North Llano River. At this stretch, the river curved north, away from the road, then west for several miles, before turning back south and rejoining the road. Luke found an opening in the brush and turned into it. He rode for a bit more than a quarter mile, until he reached the river. He rode along the bank until he located a deeper stretch of water. "Here's where we spend the night," he said to his horses, as he swung down from the saddle.

As always, Luke took care of his horses before himself. He took the gear off them, gave each a piece of licorice, then took a currycomb from his saddlebags. He used that to remove as much dirt and lathered sweat from their coats as he could. That done, he turned them loose, since neither would stray far from him. The tired animals went to the river and took a drink, then settled to cropping at the grass along the riverbank.

Luke removed an oilskin wrapped bar of harsh yellow lye soap from his saddlebags. He walked to the edge of the river, where he unbuckled his gun belt and set it in the grass. He sat down, and took off his boots, socks, bandanna, and hat. His ankles and calves were covered in welts and insect bites. Fleas jumped from Luke's skin, and he brushed off a number of bedbugs. He could feel lice crawling through his hair. Luke stood back up, and started to peel out of his shirt. He hesitated, and looked around. He laughed at himself.

"What the hell am I thinkin', worrying that someone might come by and see me buck naked? I'm out here in the middle of nowhere," he said to himself, shaking his head. He finished taking off the shirt, tossed it next to his boots, then let his denims and drawers drop. As soon they hit the dirt, he entered the water in a long, shallow dive. He swam back and forth from bank to bank several times, then retrieved the bar of soap and stood in the shallows near the bank. He lathered up, first washing his face, then covering the hair on his head. Then he continued soaping his body, covering his neck and torso with a thick coating of soap. He left the soap on for a few minutes, then scrubbed himself thoroughly. He got back in the water to rinse off, then repeated his actions twice more. He then took his clothes, soaked them in the river, and scrubbed them against the rocks, using the same bar of soap to cover every seam thickly. He took his bandanna to scrub the inside of his hat, then the insides of his boots. He set the hat and boots aside to dry, then rinsed out the rest of his clothes and laid them on the rocky riverbank to dry in the hot sun. He then sat down in the shallows, where the water reached to just below his chest, and scrubbed himself once more, to kill any insects which might have survived his first scrubbings, or which might have jumped onto him from his clothes. He rinsed off, and soaked for a while longer, letting the refreshing water soothe away the aches of the trail. Finally, he got out of the river, and stretched out in the shade of a cottonwood tree to take a nap. His horses, having filled their bellies, quit grazing, walked into the river, and laid down, gaining relief from the heat and tormenting flies.

Luke awakened about an hour before dusk. He redressed, then removed a length of string and attached fishhook from his saddlebags. He tied the string to a broken-off mesquite branch, caught a grasshopper, and attached it to the hook. He only had to wait a minute before a good-sized catfish took the bait. Luke pulled the plump fish out of the water.

"You're gonna be a mighty nice change from bacon and beans," he said to the fish. Luke cleaned his catch, placed it in his frying pan, then built a small fire from pieces of driftwood. The catfish was soon sizzling in the pan, along with some corn meal.

"Soon as I have my supper, we're gonna hit the trail again," Luke called to his horses. "Dunno how much it'll cool down tonight, but it's bound to be easier travelin' that durin' the day."

• • •

Luke generally preferred traveling at night, especially in the summer. The temperature usually dropped considerably on the high plains or in the desert. The roads were less crowded, too. So far, he had only met one pair of east-bound freighters, the heavy wagons pulled by teams of six mules. The main disadvantages to riding through the night were the increased chances for renegades to waylay and rob, even murder, unwary passersby. And for a lawman like Luke, it gave an outlaw intent on a drygulching more advantage to lie in wait, undetected, until his victim rode within range of his gun. The nighttime shadows also sometimes made horses more easily spooked; however, Luke's were used to being on the move during the dark. They were sure-footed mounts, so Luke wasn't worried about them making a misstep, possibly injuring themselves or their rider . . . or worse.

From the position of the stars, and the thin crescent moon, Luke calculated the time was nearing midnight. The land had gotten more rugged as he continued westward, still mostly level, but punctuated by the occasional low hill or mesa, slashed by shallow dry washes and deeper arroyos. Luke was riding past one of these when a silent figure leapt from the wash, grabbing at RePete's reins. The big paint shied and reared, striking out with his front hooves. His sudden move sent Luke flying from the saddle. In the split-second before he hit the ground, Luke heard the sickening crunch of bone, then a sound much like that of a melon being dropped and breaking open, when RePete's left front hoof smashed in the attacker's skull. Luke hit the road hard, landing on his back. Pain shot through him, and he lost all the air from his lungs. He heard a thud, then a scream of agony, followed by a long moan. That sound was the last thing Luke remembered before he passed out.

Luke was awakened by something warm and moist running over his face, as well as a sharp, repeating pain in his ribs. He opened his eyes when the pain hit again. RePete was swiping his long pink tongue over his rider's face, while Pete was pawing at his side. Pete placed his muzzle against Luke's side and shoved, hard. He and RePete nickered at the stunned Ranger.

"All right, dammit. I'm awake," Luke cursed. "Are you two tryin' to finish what those hombres started? Lemme get up, will ya?"

Luke struggled to his feet. To his relief, no bones seemed to be broken. He would be stiff and sore for a while, but he'd still be able to ride. He checked on the two men who'd attempted to steal his horses, and probably kill him.

"Can't even tell this hombre had a face," he muttered, looking at the man who had grabbed

RePete's reins. The horse's hoof had completely ruined his skull. He walked over to the second man, who was curled up on his side, blood running copiously from his mouth and ears. His shirt was torn open, revealing a livid bruise and cuts on his belly. Pete's hoof had caught him just above his pants' waistband. He looked up at Luke through glazed eyes.

"What'd you and your pardner think you were doin'?" Luke asked. The man opened his mouth, but no words came out, only more blood. His eyes opened wide, his body stiffened, then went slack.

"You ain't gonna talk? I reckon I already know the answer. You picked the wrong victim. My horses don't allow anybody but me to handle 'em, unless I say so. And I can't be killed that easy."

Both men were swarthy and dark featured, quite possibly full Mexicans, or half-breeds.

"Nothin' I can do for 'em, but leave 'em for the scavengers," Luke said. He gathered up his horses' reins, and pulled himself back into the saddle. "Might as well make a few more miles before sunup."

5

Luke was still sore from the fall from his horse the night before, so he found a place to camp shortly after sunrise. He rested the entire day, and slept through the night. A northerly breeze had sprung up, pushing out the humidity, and making the sun's heat at least bearable. He readied his horses, mounted Pete, and turned southwest, away from the road. From here to Alpine, he would travel cross country. Water and way stations would be harder to find, but Luke had years of experience riding off the beaten path. He'd also learned much from an Apache scout named Desert Wind. He'd taught Luke how to find water, stay hidden, and track far better than any white man could. More than once, Desert Wind's lessons had saved Luke's life.

"The next rough patch we'll hit is crossin' the Pecos, pard," Luke said to Pete, as they moved along at a steady lope. "You never know what that river might throw at us. But that's still two days off. No need to worry about it now."

Luke made good time that day. In late afternoon, he reined Pete in at a rough wooden signpost, which was stuck in the ground at the junction of a narrow side trail.

"Taylortown, one half mile," Luke read to his

horses. "Never heard of the place, but that's not surprising. New towns are poppin' up all the time out here. Most of 'em last a year or two, then fade away when folks realize this territory ain't much good for farming. Not anything else, neither, except cattle ranchin', which is always a gamble. Reckon we'll swing by and check the place out. Mebbe it'll have a stable where you two can have stalls for the night. With even more luck, there'll be a hotel where I can get a room and meal. One thing the town'll probably have is a saloon where I can get a couple of beers, to cut the trail dust from my throat. Let's go find out."

He turned Pete to the left, down the narrow trail. Ten minutes later, he rode into what claimed to be Taylortown, but which in reality was nothing more than a collection of a few hastily thrown together buildings. There was a general store, a café, a saloon, a blacksmith's shop, and a small church, along with a few small dwellings. They were constructed of green lumber, which had shrunk and warped under the Texas sun, leaving gaps between the planks. None of them were painted. The settlement had no boardwalks, not even any wooden awnings in front of the three businesses. There was no sign of a livery stable. The few people walking about eyed Luke suspiciously as he rode down the hamlet's single street. Every one of them was Black.

This must be one of those Black settlements that

have been poppin' up, Luke thought. *These folks are most likely either freed slaves who drifted west after the War, or mebbe with a few freemen from up North who drifted west to seek better lives mixed in.*

"Seems as if it might not have been worth the detour, boys," Luke said to his horses. He sighed. "Well, if nothin' else, mebbe I can rustle up some grub for me and buy some more grain for you fellas."

Luke paused at a horse trough in front of the store, to allow his horses a drink. Then he rode across the street, reined up in front of the café, and dismounted. He looped the tired animals' reins around the hitch rail, and went inside.

Three men were at the café's counter, working on their meals. They turned, stared at Luke, then went back to eating. The young Black woman behind the counter fixed Luke with a steady glare. She was slim and pretty, but the scowl on her face detracted from her looks. She had her hands on her hips.

"What you lookin' for, Mister?" Her voice was decidedly unfriendly.

"I was hopin' to find a meal, mebbe even a place to stable my horses and get a room for the night," Luke answered.

"Don't you be givin' me no tall tale, Mister. No one comes to Taylortown, particularly not no white folks. That sign's only for those on their way to settle here. Why don't you just turn around, walk on out that door, get on the horse what brung you, and ride on outta here?"

"I'll do just that," Luke said. "But you might want to take down the sign pointing folks this way, if you don't want any visitors. I'm just passin' through, and that sign caught my attention."

An older man emerged from the kitchen. He was balding, and a bit on the pudgy side. Alongside him was a woman of about the same age. She was still slim for her age, her café au lait color skin had only a few laugh creases around her eyes. Her hair had only the slightest trace of gray.

"Lucille, don't you be chasin' off any payin' customers just because they ain't colored folks," the man said. "Mister, don't pay no mind to my daughter. She thinks most all white men are no good pieces of trash. Sometimes, I think she might be right. If you ain't lookin' for trouble, you're more than welcome to sit down and break bread. I'm Eustis Taylor. I own this here café. Also the general store, and the saloon. I'm also the mayor, and the preacher on Sunday. This here's my wife, Hildy. My son Josiah is still clerkin', over at the store. It don't close for another hour."

"Luke Caldwell. Mr. Taylor. Is the town named after your family?"

"Yep. Bein' as me and my wife Hildy started it, we reckoned we had the right to name it after ourselves," Taylor answered, with a hearty laugh. "Of course, it's not much, but it's home. Me and my family were slaves on a Mississippi plantation. After Mr. Lincoln said we was free, then the War was over, we lit a shuck west fast as we could. Bought this piece of land that nobody else wanted. Everyone who lives here is either a Taylor, kin, or friends. You?"

"Like I told your daughter, I'm just passin' through on my way to West Texas. Saw the sign for Taylortown. Figured since it was gettin' on in the day, I'd swing by and see if there was a place where me'n my horses could spend the night."

"Well, you probably noticed we ain't got a hotel," Taylor answered. "No livery stable, neither. But you're welcome to put your animals in the town corral at the end of the street, and roll out your blankets behind that if you're of a mind to. As far as supper, we don't have much on the menu, but my wife ain't a bad cook at all, and she bakes a mean sweet tater pie. After we close up the café at seven, we open the saloon, if you're of a mind for somethin' a bit stronger than coffee, or chicory tea."

"That sounds good to me, Mr. Taylor," Luke said. He took a back corner table.

"Well, go ahead, Lucille. Wait on the man," her father ordered.

45

Lucille made a face, then shrugged. She walked over to Luke's table.

"What're you havin', Mister?" she asked, her voice still surly.

"Depends on what you've got," Luke answered. "What would you suggest?"

"We've got chitlins, fatback pork, beef stew, and blackeyed peas. If I was you, I'd go with the chitlins and stew."

"Sounds good."

"Cornbread or biscuits?"

"Both."

"Coffee or chicory?"

"Coffee, black. You can bring the pot."

"Anythin' else?"

"Save me a big slice of your ma's sweet potato pie. Two, if it's as good as your pa claims. Oh, and a smile."

"A what?"

"A smile. I see too many frowning faces in my travels. I'll bet you have a real pretty smile."

Despite herself, Lucille managed a slight smile.

"See, that's much better," Luke said.

"I'll be right back with your coffee."

Lucille turned and stalked into the kitchen. The three men at the counter laughed.

After finishing his supper, Luke went to the Taylortown Saloon. He had two beers, and ordered a third. The beer, as he had expected, was warm, but at least it was wet, and not too weak. Taylor had just set a full mug in front of Luke when a woman outside began screaming, followed by the loud voices of men arguing. Another woman's voice joined the cacophony of screams and yells. A man yelped in pain, followed by the thud of a body hitting the ground.

"That's Hildy and Lucille!" Taylor exclaimed. He reached under the bar and came up with an old Remington sawed-off shotgun.

"Better let me take a hand in this, Eustis," Luke said. "This is my line of work."

He pulled his Peacemaker from its holster, and hurried outside.

Josiah Taylor was lying in the middle of the road, unconscious. Two white men were holding Hildy back, while a third was dragging Lucille toward the narrow space between the store and a residence.

"Let go of those women!" Luke shouted. The men looked at him in disbelief.

"This ain't none of your business, stranger, whoever you are. If you know what's good for you, you'll head on outta town," the oldest of the three said. He tightened his grip on Hildy's arm. "Rufus, you just go ahead and have your fun. Me'n Caleb'll make sure this yahoo don't interfere."

"That's where you're wrong," Luke said.

"Yeah? How you gonna stop us? You damn

sure can't try'n shoot us. You'd be more likely to plug one of the women if you tried. Nigger," he continued to Taylor, "you'd best keep yourself and your shotgun outta the situation, too. Unless you want to kill your own kin. We ain't gonna hurt 'em, I promise. My boys just want to see what it's like to have a darky woman. Oh, and since you didn't take our warnin' to pack up and go back where you come from, we're gonna burn you out."

"The Devil you will, Lucius Jones," Taylor retorted.

"And I'm makin' it my business," Luke added.

"You're makin' a big mistake," Jones said. "Seems me'n my boys are holdin' all the high cards. Not much you can do."

Luke hesitated. It appeared Jones was right. He didn't dare attempt to shoot him or his sons, for fear of his bullet striking one of the women instead. The Joneses could also easily maim or kill Hildy or Lucille with their bare hands. They didn't appear to be carrying any firearms, but they probably had guns, or at least knives, somewhere on their persons. Luke made his decision. He shoved his six-gun back in its holster.

"I reckon you win this pot."

Jones threw back his head and laughed. As he did, Luke lunged at Rufus. He lowered his shoulders and slammed into the young man's ribs, breaking his grip on Lucille. Luke's momentum carried both men to the ground. Luke landed on his back. Rufus drove his knee into Luke's gut. Luke struggled to regain his lost air. He managed to toss the heavier, younger man aside, avoiding a knockout punch to his jaw. Luke scrambled to his feet, grabbed Rufus by his shirtfront, and pulled him upright. Still hanging on to Rufus's shirt, Luke shot two quick jabs to his belly, then an uppercut to the point of Rufus's chin. The much patched, almost paper thin fabric of Rufus's shirt tore. When he toppled backwards, he used his legs as a scythe to cut Luke's out from under him as he fell. He shot a kick to Luke's ribs. Both men got back on their feet. Luke again ducked a vicious punch aimed at his head, then slammed three quick punches to Rufus's belly. The impacts barely elicited a grunt from Luke's adversary. Then, Rufus launched a punch that didn't miss its target. The blow took Luke directly on the point of his chin, snapping his head back. His arms dropped, leaving him defenseless from a powerful left and right to his gut. Luke jackknifed, staggered. He managed to bring himself upright, only to take another punch to his jaw. He toppled like a felled oak, landing hard on his back. He lay there, gasping like a fish out of water, his head spinning. Blood filled his mouth.

"You got him now, little brother," Caleb shouted. "Finish him off."

"Make certain of him for good," Lucius ordered.

Rufus looked at his brother and father. He grinned. Luke knew if the youngest Jones landed one more punch, it would be all over for him. In desperation, as Rufus moved in for the killing blow, Luke rammed his boot heel directly into Rufus's groin. Rufus howled in agony, grabbed his crotch, doubled over, and staggered into a hitch rail. The rail broke in two and collapsed under Rufus as he fell.

"Caleb, get that son of a bitch," Lucius ordered. "Kill the damn bastard."

"I'll take care of him, Pa."

Caleb was even bigger than his younger brother. Luke knew he didn't stand a chance against him in a fistfight, even if he weren't as battered as he was right now. He grabbed a section of the broken rail when Caleb charged. He drove the splintered end of the rail deep into Caleb's stomach, the jagged wood tearing through Caleb's shirt, piercing his flesh, penetrating muscle, the needle sharp splinters stopping only after they had punctured Caleb's stomach. When he buckled, Luke swung the rail in a vicious arc, slamming it into the side of Caleb's skull. Caleb crumpled in a heap.

Lucius, seeing his two sons down, bellowed like a bull. He shoved Hildy to the road, then took a knife from a sheath hidden behind his shirt. Luke pulled out his revolver.

"Drop that knife right now, old man, or all six bullets in this gun are goin' right into your belly," he ordered. "Don't think I'd hesitate one minute to fill your guts fulla lead."

Lucius paused in mid-stride. Seeing the determination in Luke's eyes, he realized the Ranger meant exactly what he said. If Lucius took one more step, he'd be a dead man. With a vicious curse, he threw down his knife.

Hildy and Lucille were hugging in the middle of the street.

"You ladies all right?" Luke asked.

Hildy nodded.

"Better check on your boy. See if you can bring him around. Eustis, keep your gun on that hombre, while I check on his two sorry excuses for sons," Luke ordered.

"He makes a move and I'll blow him to Kingdom Come," Taylor assured the Ranger.

Caleb had regained consciousness. He was holding one hand to his stomach, the other to the profusely bleeding split-open skin on his scalp. His eyes were glassy. He lay moaning.

"You must have even a thicker skull than I thought," Luke told him. "I figured for certain I caved it in. Next time I'll make certain."

"Next time . . . things'll turn out . . . different," Caleb gasped.

"We'll see."

Luke turned to Rufus, who was still lying

51

curled up on his side. He was whimpering.

"You done crushed my man parts," he complained.

"I sure hope so," Luke answered. "I reckon you won't be tryin' to violate any more women anytime soon . . . if ever."

"Pa. Pa, this hombre ruined my nuts," Rufus called to his father, his voice cracking. "Ain't ya gonna do somethin' about it?"

"Not with a shotgun pointed at my back. You should've done it your ownself, while you had the chance, you useless sack of . . ."

Luke cut Lucius off.

"No cussin'. There are ladies present."

"What ladies? Hell, I don't see nothin' but colored trash."

Luke walked up to Lucius and slapped him across the face, so hard he broke the skin on his left cheek and split his lips open.

"The only trash here is you and your whelps," Luke said. "You're all under arrest. I'm a Texas Ranger. Name's Luke Caldwell. The charges are assault, assault on a peace officer, attempted murder, attempted murder of a peace officer, threatening, and assorted others, which means anything else I can think of."

"You'll never make those charges stick, Ranger. That is, if you even live long enough to get us to the county seat. We ain't hardly licked yet," Lucius snapped. "And even if you do get us there, ain't no jury in Texas gonna convict white folks of attackin' a bunch of damn useless niggers."

Most of the residents of Taylortown had come out of their houses. A murmur ran through the crowd. Several men suggested getting a rope.

"There'll be no lynching, y'all hear?" Luke said. "I'll arrest any man who tries that."

The grumbling grew louder.

"Just hold on," Eustis said. "Time to let cooler heads prevail. The Ranger's right. If we lynch these men, it'll only turn out the worse for us. You know that's a fact."

"My husband's speakin' the truth, and y'all know it," Hildy added. Josiah was now standing alongside her and his sister. He had a broken nose, and a bloodied right ear. "Let the Ranger handle the Joneses. If we take the law into our own hands, we'll be no better than them."

"He's probably just gonna turn 'em loose anyway," someone in the crowd shouted.

"I don't work that way," Luke said. "I *will* take them in for trial. You have my promise on that."

"Yeah, but Luke, unfortunately, Jones is right," Eustis said. "They'll be turned loose, probably before you're even out of town."

"Not with the charges of assault and attempted murder of a peace officer," Luke objected.

"They'll merely claim they didn't know you were a Ranger, and they were just defendin' themselves. They'll get away with it."

"So you're sayin' you want me to just turn these hombres loose, Eustis?"

"No. I'm sayin' there's no other choice. It'd just be a waste of time. Besides, it seems like they've been punished enough."

"See. Even a dumb darky knows where things stand, Ranger," Lucius said, with a sneer.

Luke slugged him in the belly, then slammed his fist into Lucius's mouth when he folded. The man spit out blood, along with several pieces of broken teeth.

"You might want to keep your mouth closed, Jones. I'm just itchin' for a reason to shut you up permanently. Don't tempt me."

"You just wait, you nigger-lovin' lawdog," Jones muttered.

Luke punched him in the nose, flattening it and bringing forth a fountain of blood.

"All right, mebbe now they've been punished enough," he said. "I'll let them go, on one condition. You folks hire yourself a town marshal. I know, a marshal costs money. But it would be money well spent. Besides, you could probably find a man who'd be willin' to work for grub and a roof over his head, until you could afford to pay him. Are we in agreement?"

"I reckon," Eustis said. "We cain't keep on like this, that's for certain."

"Then it's settled. Jones, you and your boys are free to go. But if I ever find out you've been botherin' the people of this town again, next time I *will* bring you in, and I'll make certain you spend a long time behind bars, or hang. Now get outta here."

"You ain't seen the last of us, Ranger," Lucius threatened. His words were slurred from his swollen lips, broken teeth, and blood filled mouth.

"I hope not. I purely hope not. I'm ready to finish our little set-to anytime you're ready."

"Caleb, Rufus, get up," Lucius ordered. "We'll finish with this Ranger another day."

"Pa, I don't think I can even walk as far as my horse, let alone set a saddle," Rufus whined, after he struggled to his feet. He stood spraddle-legged. "I hurt somethin' awful. Everythin' between my legs is all swole up."

"I ain't feelin' too good, neither," Caleb added. "But I can ride as far as home."

"Rufus, you'll get on your horse, and you'll ride, or I'll cut off everythin' between your legs myself," his father ordered. "You too, Caleb. Now get movin'. We need to get home and tend to our hurts. Rufus, your brother's liable to bleed out if we don't."

Lucius gave Rufus a rough shove.

"Nice neighbors you've got there, Eustis," Luke said, as the Joneses stumbled toward the end of the street. Their horses were tied to a clump of mesquites at the edge of town, explaining why

Luke hadn't heard them ride in. "How long have those brutes been botherin' you?"

"We can talk inside the house," Hildy said. "Luke and Josiah need their wounds treated."

"I can patch myself up," Luke said. "Been hurt far worse'n this, many times."

"Nonsense. Those wounds are liable to get infected, and give you blood poisoning, especially considering how filthy those Joneses keep themselves. They ain't had a bath in at least six months, probably longer."

"Hildy's right," a woman said. "Me'n my sister Sue will give you a hand, if you'd like, Hildy."

"We'd be obliged, Martha. Don't you argue with me, Ranger," Hildy said, when Luke started to protest.

"I've never won an argument with my wife yet," Eustis said, with a chuckle. "Cain't think of anyone who ever has. There's no use in you tryin'. You won't win."

"All right," Luke said. "I've got some questions for you folks anyway. I can ask 'em while we're gettin' patched up."

They headed inside the Taylors' small house. While Lucille and Martha fussed over Josiah, Hildy and Sue tended to Luke's injuries. They had already started heating water to make a poultice to cover both men's scrapes and bruises. Over Luke's objections, Hildy had forced him to remove his shirt. His abdomen and ribs were one massive bruise.

"Keep watch out that window, Eustis, and keep your shotgun handy, just in case Jones and his boys are dumb enough to try'n come back," Luke ordered.

"I'll make mincemeat of 'em if they do," Taylor promised.

"I'm gonna ask you a few questions now, if you don't mind."

"Ranger, as long as you keep still and don't go wigglin' around whilst I'm fixin' you up, you can ask all the questions you want," Hildy said.

"It's a deal. First, I've got to ask Lucille how this all started. Take your time, and if it's too upsetting, just say so."

"It was scary, but Rufus and Caleb Jones are not gonna ruin my life," Lucille answered. "Before I start, though, I have to apologize for misjudging you. And thank you for saving me from them. Lord knows what they would have done."

"Child, you know exactly what their intentions were. Their pa's too," Hildy broke in.

"You're right, Ma. I do," Lucille conceded. "Anyway, Ranger, after the café closed, we walked over to the store to meet my brother. Then we started to walk home together, like we do most every night. Usually there's a few townsfolk about, and that's all. So we never worried about bein' safe."

"You mean the Joneses had never bothered you before?"

"They'd come around and made threats to my folks, and talked nasty to me, but that was as far as it went, until tonight," Lucile explained. "They surprised us by hiding in the alley, then jumping out. My poor brother didn't have a chance against them."

"Hey, I got in a couple of good licks, Sis," Josiah objected. "I might've been able to handle one of 'em, but not all three."

"I know, Josiah, and you were real brave. You bought enough time for Pa and the Ranger to get out and take a hand. If you hadn't, it might've been too late."

"Only wish I could have done more," Josiah said.

"You saw the rest, Ranger," Lucille continued. "They nearly beat Josiah to death, then Rufus tried to drag me off. If you and my Pa hadn't come out when you did . . ."

"You don't need to say anythin' more," Luke said, stopping her short. "Eustis, tell me all you can about the Joneses. Where'd they come from? Who settled here first, you or them? Have they got any kinfolk in the area?"

"From what I hear tell, they came to Texas from the hills of eastern Kentucky. I reckon the folks beck there were glad to be shut of 'em. They settled here about two or three years before I bought the land Taylortown sets on. I understand Jones's wife, the boys' mother, came with 'em, but she disappeared a few months later. Some folks claim she pulled up stakes and went back to Kentucky. Others say she was murdered by Lucius. I tend to believe those."

"Them boys and their father are awful mean," Lucille said.

"My sister's right," Josiah agreed. "They throw their weight around, and bully anyone who crosses 'em."

"They've made a pact with the Devil. Sold their souls to Satan," Hildy added. "They've got everyone around these parts plumb scared to death of who they'll come after next."

"Do they think your land should belong to them?" Luke asked.

"They think anythin' they want belongs to 'em," Eustis answered.

"That means they meant what they said about burnin' you folks out. It also means they'll try again," Luke said.

"It does," Eustis confirmed. "And sooner or later, they will."

"Why hasn't anyone called the law?"

"Hell, Ranger, there ain't no law in these parts. You're the first lawman we've seen in months. And you'll be movin' on, come mornin'. Pardon my cussin', Hildy."

"Besides, no white lawman's gonna take the

side of us colored folk," Josiah said, hate and frustration plain in his voice.

"I just did," Luke pointed out.

"I reckon you did, at that," Josiah conceded. "That still won't do us any good once you ride out, though."

"Where is the Jones place? I reckon I might pay 'em a call on my way out of town."

"You won't have to look for the Joneses," Eustis said. "After what happened today, they'll be lookin' for you. And sure as shootin', they'll find you. If you're headin' west, you've got to go right past their place anyway. It's a rundown old farm, just past when you turned off for town. Story is they never actually bought the place, just moved in after findin' it abandoned. They've been squattin' there ever since. They don't seem to do much farming. Since, besides Taylortown, it's the only place for another twenty miles in either direction, they put up travelers who make the mistake of stoppin' there. Most of 'em are relieved of any valuables while they sleep. If they try'n get their stuff back, they either leave in lot worse shape than when they arrived, or don't leave at all."

"I reckon I'll have to put a stop to their little enterprise," Luke said.

"You cain't handle those three by yourself," Lucille protested.

"This time I won't be countin' on just my fists,"

Luke said. "I'll be relyin' on Mr. Sam Colt's help."

"Hildy, here's the poultice," Sue said. She held a bowl which contained a foul smelling, greenish substance.

"Thanks, child. Ranger, you keep still, whilst I smear this here potion over your belly and ribs. Then the rest'll go on the cuts and bruises on your face. It smells awful, and stings somethin' fierce, but it'll knock down the swelling, and pull the poisons out of those wounds. You'll feel a lot better by morning."

Luke wrinkled his nose.

"What's in it?"

"A mess of herbs and roots. It's a concoction I brought from Mississippi. It's harder to find the plants I need out here in Texas, but I've managed. Hold still now."

Hildy took a handful of the poultice, slapped it on Luke's belly, then spread it over his skin. Luke winced. He stiffened, then settled back as the potion's sting cooled to a soothing warmth.

"How's that feel, Ranger?" Hildy asked.

"Like someone rubbed chili peppers all over my gut," Luke said.

"That means it's working. Soon as you're patched up, we'll call it a night."

"The Joneses might come back," Luke pointed out.

"Not after the whuppin' you laid on 'em," Eustis

61

said. "They'll lay low and lick their wounds for a few days. But me'n Josiah will keep watch, just in case. You get your rest. You're gonna need it, if you intend to call on Lucius Jones and his boys."

Sue returned, holding a steaming mug. She handed that to Luke.

"You need to drink this sassafras tea, Ranger," she said. "It's very soothing. Hildy always keeps some ready to brew for anyone who might become ill, or gets hurt."

"It sure smells good," Luke said. He took a sip. "Whoa! What's in this mug? It sure ain't just tea."

"It's mostly tea," Hildy said. "With a good dollop of Eustis's best corn squeezin's mixed in. Now you just sit still and drink that tea while I tend to you. You'll sleep like a baby if you do."

Luke took another swallow. He shook his head.

"I don't doubt that. It's the headache in the mornin' I'm worried about."

"You needn't be, Ranger," Eustis said. "The sassafras in Hildy's tea stops any headache. No upset stomach, neither."

"Yeah, right. *Sure* it does," Luke said. Despite his misgivings, he drained the mug. By the time Hildy finished treating his facial injuries, he was passed out.

"I reckon I'd better help you get him on the couch, Hildy," Eustis said.

"No. Me'n Sue can handle him. Lucille can lend a hand if we need her. You just make certain them Joneses ain't comin' back."

"Yeah. I'd best do that. Wouldn't do to have 'em sneak up on us in the dark."

6

When he awoke the next morning, Luke was surprised to find Hildy hadn't fibbed about her poultice and corn liquor laced tea. He was stiff and sore, yes, but not nearly as much as he would have expected. Even better, his mouth didn't feel like cotton, his stomach wasn't churning, and he had no headache whatsoever. He also had a good appetite. He ate a hearty breakfast, made his goodbyes to the Taylors, and resumed his journey about an hour after sunrise. As usual, he talked to his horses as he rode.

"I ain't lookin' forward to facing Lucius Jones and his boys this mornin', pards. Sure, I'm feelin' quite a bit better after Hildy's so called 'tea,' but I'm still pretty damn sore. Now, I figure, with any luck, Caleb won't be able to put up much of a fight, that's if he's even still alive, but I'd wager my Stetson Lucius and Rufus still are ready, and just itchin' to finish what they started. Mebbe I can talk some reason into 'em. But I damn for certain ain't countin' on it. And I reckon if I get into another fight with 'em, I'll come out on the losin' end this time for sure. Dunno what those bastards ate when they were growin' up, but they sure grew big, and mean. I think I'll ride up on 'em with my gun already drawn, and if they try'n start anythin' just shoot 'em where they stand."

RePete turned to look at his rider, then snorted.

"No, I ain't forgotten, given the chance, they'd probably bushwhack me and be done with it, ya knothead," Luke said, laughing. "I'm countin' on you and your brother to warn me if they do."

When Luke neared the intersection with the main trail, the acrid odor of wood smoke came to his nostrils. Thin tendrils of gray smoke stained the cloudless sky, a short distance to the north and west.

"What in the blue blazes? I sure hope some damn loco fool ain't burnin' brush on a hot dry day like this. Any embers get downwind and they'll be liable to start a prairie fire that'll run for miles, and destroy anything in its path. C'mon, RePete. We'd better see what's goin' on."

He put his horses into a fast lope. It only took a few minutes to reach the source of the smoke. The burnt-out, collapsed ruins of a cabin and barn were still smoldering. The only signs of life were three emaciated horses, grazing in the brush. They had evidently broken through their corral fence to escape the flames. Luke pulled RePete to a halt.

"From the location Eustis gave me, this has gotta be the Jones place, or at least it was," Luke said to himself. "Looks like the horses they were ridin' yesterday, too. I wonder what started the fire. I'd better see if anyone's still alive in what's left of the place."

Luke dismounted, and pulled his revolver from its holster. He walked over to the blackened, smoldering wreckage of the cabin.

"Anybody still in there didn't have a chance," he muttered. "I don't see any signs of bodies, though. There should be a few bones left, if nothin' else. Mebbe they did manage to escape before the flames got too hot. I'll check what's left of the barn."

When Luke reached the barn, he heard whimpering coming from underneath a fallen section of the wall.

"Could be a person, but it sounds more like an animal. I'd better try'n get it outta there. Might have to shoot it and put it out of its misery, but that'd still be better'n leaving it trapped, to suffer until it burns to death, or of thirst or starvation from bein' trapped."

Luke squatted on his haunches, and lifted the seared edge of the boards. As soon as he did, a puppy, about six months old, scrambled out. It jumped at the Ranger, puts its front paws on Luke's shoulders, and started furiously licking his face, while yelping with relief and joy.

"Whoa! Easy there, feller," Luke said. "Don't drown me before I have a chance to see if you're hurt, and might need some medicating."

He pushed the pup back, holding it at arm's length.

"Sure enough, you've got some of the hair singed off your ears and tail, boy. Looks like the pads of your feet got burned, too. But you should be all right, once I fix you up. Appears like you could use a good feedin', too. You're doggone skinny. I can see every one of your ribs, and your hip bones are stickin' out. You've got a couple of nasty bruises, too, seems like. Looks like the Joneses mistreated you, too. And those horses over yonder."

Luke picked up the puppy and carried him over to where his own horses waited.

"You just stay put, whilst I dig out some ointment to slather over those burns," Luke said. The puppy sat, his gaze never leaving Luke while the Ranger rummaged in his saddlebags and pulled out a jar of salve. He hunkered on his heels, to coat the pup's burns with the medicine. Before Luke even made the attempt, the puppy rolled onto his back, his feet up in the air. He whined, as if asking Luke to cover his paws with the medicine. Luke laughed.

"Well, if you ain't a smart critter."

He treated the pup's paws, then replaced the jar of salve in his saddlebags, and took out several strips of jerky. He lifted his canteen from the saddle horn, poured half its contents in his hat, and let the pup drink its fill. Once it was done drinking, Luke gave him the jerky, which the pup eagerly gulped down. He wagged his tail and whined again, looking for more.

"Not right now, feller," Luke said. "Too much might upset your stomach. Now I've gotta figure out what to do with you. I can't leave you here, that's for certain. But you sure can't run alongside me, not until those paws are healed up. You reckon you'll be able to ride across my saddle, until I can rig somethin' up for you?"

The pup barked, then stared toward a clump of cottonwoods and live oaks. He began growling at a shadow in the midst of the trees, which was swaying in the slight breeze. Concentrating on the ruins of the buildings, Luke hadn't noticed whatever the pup was now barking at. The hackles on its neck stood straight up. Luke took a closer look at what had caught the pup's attention.

"Damn! That's a body. Appears as if someone's been strung up."

Keeping his six-gun at the ready, Luke walked over to the small grove. The pup stuck with him, growling and barking. Luke stopped short when he reached the trees.

"I guess I don't have to worry about Lucius Jones and his boys after all. Not any more. Someone got to 'em before I did."

Lucius, Caleb, and Rufus's bodies were festooning the limbs of a live oak, appearing as some sort of macabre Christmas ornaments. A sign was pinned to Lucius's shirt.

"Guilty of murder, robbery, beatings, and attacking women," Luke read.

"I probably should try'n figure out who hung these hombres, but I ain't got the time," he muttered. "Besides, I reckon I know who did it. Eustis Taylor and some of the men from Taylortown must've decided to take the law into their own hands. Came over here in the middle of the night while they Taylors weren't expecting them. Probably figured they were hurt too bad to put up much of a fight, and this was their chance to get shut of 'em once and for all. Appears as if Caleb might've already been dead before they hung him. If not, he was damn close to it. Now I know why Hildy and Eustis gave me that corn liquor laced tea. They wanted to make certain I stayed passed out until after Eustis and the men with him got back home. With no witnesses, there's no way of connectin' 'em to this lynching. Can't say as I blame them. And I guess justice was served, even if it wasn't in a court of law. This ain't the first time it's happened, and it won't be the last."

Caleb's shirt, where Luke had driven the splintered section of hitch rail into his stomach, was soaked with half dried blood. There was no expression of fear on his face, unlike his father and brother. Plainly, he had been unconscious, or dead, at the moment of his hanging.

"Nothin' more I can do here, except say a prayer that these hombres repented of their wicked ways before they met their Maker, and that He'll have mercy on their souls."

Luke removed his hat, bowed his head, and said a silent prayer. He finished by making the Sign of the Cross. While Luke was a Baptist, as were the majority of Anglos in Texas, he had picked up the gesture while riding with the Rangers along the Rio Grande, where most of the population was folks with Mexican blood, and were Catholics. Somehow, the simple prayer reminded Luke that the Lord was always near.

"Let's get outta here, boy," Luke said to the pup. "I'm guessin' these hombres treated you as bad as they treated everyone they came across."

Luke picked up the pup, and walked back to his horses. He placed the pup across the seat of his saddle, then climbed up behind him.

"I know it ain't the most comfortable way to ride, but it'll have to do until we make camp for the night, feller," Luke told the pup. "And we dang sure can't stay here. Those horses are on their own. They're better off turnin' wild, rather than being abused by the Joneses. Besides, I have a feelin', once he's certain I've ridden off, Eustis and his son will come back and claim those broncs for themselves. Can't say as I blame them. Least they could get, after what they and their town have been puttin' up with."

The puppy stretched its neck as far as he could, and licked Luke's face. Luke laughed, and scratched the pup's ears.

"All right, let's get movin'."

He heeled RePete into a walk.

Luke made camp shortly after sundown. After caring for his animals, and fixing his own supper, he rolled out his blankets and slid under them. The pup curled up alongside him.

"I guess I should give you a name, until I figure out what to do with you," he said. The pup was mostly white, with brown ears and patches on his head, a brown patch on his rump, and an entirely brown tail, except for a white tip.

"Tippy? No, doesn't suit you. Smoky? Nope. You're not smoke colored. I've got it. Blaze. You like that one?"

The pup thumped his tail on the ground.

"Good. Then Blaze it is."

Blaze licked Luke's face.

"There's no need to drown me," Luke spluttered. "We've got to cross the Pecos in two or three days. If we ain't careful, that damn river'll drown us for certain anyway. Get some sleep. Once your feet heal up, you'll have to start usin' 'em. Don't get any ideas about my lap bein' a permanent perch."

Blaze put his head between his front legs, sighed, and closed his eyes. Luke lay for quite a while, staring up at the stars. It bothered him that he hadn't seen any way to arrest anyone from Taylortown for the Joneses' lynchings. True, there was no question of the Joneses' guilt, but they should have been tried and convicted in a court of law, not by vigilante justice. However, in one thing both Lucius Jones and Eustis Taylor were correct. There was not a jury in Texas that would bring a conviction of a White man against a Black. Even though it stuck in Luke's craw, perhaps this was the only way justice could be served. With that thought, he drifted off to sleep.

7

Luke had rigged up a makeshift carrier from one of his blankets for Blaze to ride in. He hung it from the side of his packsaddle. The dog took to the sack like a duck to water. He rode in it happily, watching the passing scenery, barking when he spotted a jackrabbit, roadrunner, or other animal. Two and a half days later, by mid-afternoon, they reached the steep banks of the Pecos River.

"Damn. The river's runnin' high," Luke said, looking at the rapidly moving water. Ripples and rapids indicated hidden rocks or snags. "We're gonna have to swim it, boys," he told his horses, and his dog. "There's no possible way we'll find a decent ford. Not that there's many on this river anyhow. Besides, with the river bein' in flood, we might be better off havin' to swim it anyway. Less chance of boggin' down in the mud, or getting sucked under by quicksand. I'll let you fellers rest awhile while I ponder the situation."

The Pecos River, which took a winding route from New Mexico southeast through Texas, with many horseshoe bends and changes of direction, often backing up on itself en route to the Rio Grande. It emptied into the Rio a few miles northwest of Seminole Canyon. Crossing it at virtually any point along its entire length was extremely hazardous. The fast currents were unpredictable, and no ferries crossed it. There were unseen drop-offs, hidden underwater rocks and snags that could entangle and drown a horse or man, along with sandy soils that might look perfectly safe, but which instead could be deadly quicksand. In addition, the banks were steep, forcing a horse and rider to slide down them, and plunge into the silt laden water. Then, if the crossing was successful, the climb out of the river was just as steep, forcing a man's mount to struggle to reach safe, solid ground.

The Pecos was so notorious that it had only one well-traveled ford, miles north of Luke's position. Even that ford was so dangerous it was named Horsehead Crossing, after the bleached skulls of horses and mules mounted on trees on either side of the Pecos. Those animals, along with cattle, and many men, had died attempting to ford the river, either from drowning, or being poisoned by drinking the brackish, alkaline water.

Luke swung out of his saddle. He lifted Blaze from his carrier and set him down. The pup raced for the nearest tree.

"Both of you relax for a spell, while I look over the situation," he said to his horses. He loosened their cinches and slid the bits from their mouths, so they could crop at the sparse grass and vegetation, while he studied the roiling river.

Luke spent over a half hour studying the currents, whirlpools, and eddies of the raging Pecos. He was considering swimming across one stretch of deeper, quieter water, until a fallen tree caught in the current disappeared under the surface, then reappeared several hundred yards downstream, trapped in a whirlpool. It swirled around and around, the current giving no sign it would free its trapped victim.

"Must be quite an undertow," Luke muttered. "It'd drag me'n the horses under for certain. That kills one idea."

Unlike most cowboys, the majority of whom couldn't swim, and had an innate fear of deep water, Luke was a capable swimmer. He continued searching for a relatively safe crossing. He finally decided on a section about a hundred yards upriver, where the banks weren't quite as steep. His horses should be able to handle the descent into the Pecos without having to slide down on their haunches. The opposite bank would be a relatively easy climb out . . . if Luke and his animals didn't go under mid-river and drown. Whether or not the current would overpower them was the big unknown.

"Smartest thing to do would be wait a day or two, and see if the water drops, Blaze," he said to the pup, who sat watching Luke expectantly. "Problem is, there's no way to know if the river's still risin', or it's reached its crest, and is gonna start fallin'. There's no high water mark indicating it's started to recede. If it's still risin', it'll be too high to even attempt to cross. We could be stuck here for days. That's time we just don't have. No point in waitin' any longer."

Luke removed several lengths of rope from his saddlebags, which he used to secure prisoners. He tied those together to fasten a makeshift harness and leash for Blaze. The pup whined, and tried to pull away when Luke slid it over his head and around his shoulders.

"Sorry, feller, but you've got to get used to wearin' a leash sometimes. This is one of those times. If the river tries to pull you under, I'll hang onto you and break its grip."

Luke next retrieved his horses. He slid the bits back in their mouths, then tightened their cinches.

"I'm gonna have to swim alongside you, RePete," he said, giving the horse a leftover biscuit. "Don't want my weight to push you under."

RePete nickered. His brother Pete nuzzled at Luke's shoulder.

"Of course I've got a biscuit for you too," Luke said. "You're gonna be carryin' everything I own."

After giving Pete his treat, Luke took his bedroll and slicker from behind the cantle of his saddle. He spread the slicker on the ground, then unrolled the blankets and placed them on top. He took his Winchester from its saddle boot, and placed the rifle on the blankets. Next, he removed his gun belt, putting it on the blankets, making certain his Peacemaker was snug in its holster. That done, he pulled off his boots and clothing, stripping to the skin. He laid the clothes, and his hat, out with his weapons, then rolled the blankets and contents in his slicker, tying the bundle tightly. He lashed it to the top of the packsaddle Pete carried. Lastly, he tied his boots together, then wrapped the rope securing them around his saddle horn. He gave the rope one final tug, making certain it was tight. The last thing he'd need would be his boots sinking to the bottom of the Pecos.

"No point in wastin' any more time here. The only thing that'll accomplish is gettin' my nether regions sunburned. Sure don't need that."

He picked up Blaze's leash and swung into his saddle.

"Blaze, you stick by me, no matter what happens. RePete, soon as we hit the water, I'll slide off your back, and latch onto the stirrup. I'm countin' on you to pull me across the river. That current would most likely be a mite much for me to handle by my ownself. And if you try buckin' while I'm up here in my birthday suit, you'll be in deep trouble, horse. I'll sell you for dog food. Let's go."

He rode RePete to the edge of the riverbank, with Blaze trotting alongside, and Pete following.

"Okay, pard, let's do it."

Luke dug his heels into RePete's sides. The paint snorted, then plunged over the bank, Pete right behind him. He and Pete half walked, half slid into the river. As soon as the water was knee deep on his horses, Luke kicked his feet out of the stirrups, slipped off RePete's left side, and grabbed the stirrup. He fought to keep his grip while the horse hit deeper water, and began swimming. Luke kicked his feet, helping the horse as best he could. Blaze dog paddled strongly alongside him.

Once they neared midstream, the current grew stronger. It started pushing Luke and his animals downstream. Luke had allowed for this. The place where he planned to get out of the river was still several hundred yards downriver. He gave a brief sigh of relief when they passed the halfway point, and the current started to slacken. Just as he did, a sudden surge of water splashed over him and his animals. It knocked both horses off balance. Luke was forced under the surface when RePete rolled on top of him. He let go of the stirrup, barely avoiding the struggling horse's slashing hooves. He was jerked sideways by Blaze's pulling on his leash in his frantic efforts to avoid drowning. The pup's yank pulled Luke out from under RePete as the horse righted himself, and lunged forward. His left rear hoof struck Luke in the belly, forcing the air out of his rider's lungs. Luke swallowed a good volume of the alkaline river water. He began to sink. He made a desperate lunge for RePete's tail, latching onto it in the nick of time. The horse had righted himself, and was swimming powerfully toward the opposite shore. Luke, fighting the nausea threatening to overcome him, clung tightly to the horse's tail, and the pup's leash.

An eddy pushed Luke, his horses and dog, toward the far shore. RePete scrambled when his hooves caught purchase on an underwater sandbar. He lunged out of the Pecos and up the bank, dragging Luke and Blaze with him. A few yards upriver, Pete also emerged from the river. Both horses stopped and shook themselves. Luke let go of RePete's tail, but held on to Blaze's leash. The pup shook himself off, then came over to Luke and began licking his face. He whined. Luke tried to reassure the pup he was all right, but only managed to choke.

Luke remained lying on his belly. He gagged, and vomited violently, emptying his stomach of the large amount of water he'd swallowed. Once he'd finished retching, he coughed more water from his lungs. Exhausted, he lowered his head back to the sand. Blaze resumed licking Luke's face. He pawed at Luke's back.

"I'll be all right, boy," Luke said. He reached up to scratch Blaze's ears. "Soon as I catch my breath, I'll take care of you and the horses."

Luke rolled onto his back. He lay still for

several minutes, until he was certain he could stand without collapsing. Once he got to his feet, the first thing he did was walk over to where Pete stood, head hanging and spraddle-legged. As Luke had feared, his packsaddle had been thoroughly soaked. He uncinched the saddle and let it fall to the ground. He untied his slicker, took it off the saddle, placed it on the ground, and unrolled it. Water had seeped through the ends of the slicker, soaking everything inside. Luke swore.

"Guess I'm done travelin' for the rest of this day. I'll have to lay my clothes out in the sun to dry. That won't take long in this heat. But my guns are another story. I've got to clean and oil them before goin' any farther. I can't chance ridin' through these parts without working weapons. Just hope the river didn't ruin all my ammunition." He paused, and sighed. "First things first, though."

Luke opened his pack, and took out a small, oilskin wrapped pack of grain. He poured a portion of oats for each of his horses to eat. He opened his saddlebags, removed several strips of jerky, and tossed those to Blaze. After that, he took out a currycomb to groom his exhausted horses, while they worked on their grain. He took the gear off them, then brushed them thoroughly, using a damp rag to squeegee excess water from their coats. Only after his animals were cared for did Luke turn his attention to his own needs. He spread out his clothes to dry, along with his boots, then sat against the trunk of a stunted, struggling to survive cottonwood. He took a long drink from his canteen, then drifted off to sleep.

When Luke awakened, it was full dark. His horses, having filled their bellies on mesquite pods and leaves, were stretched out on their sides, dozing. Blaze was finishing the remains of a jackrabbit he'd caught. He looked at Luke and barked.

"I see you and your pards have filled their bellies," Luke said to him. "I'm feelin' mighty empty too. Reckon it's time to make my own supper. Soon as I get dressed."

Luke's clothes and boots were now dry. He got them back on, then buckled his gun belt around his waist. He hoped he wouldn't have to use his Colt before he got the chance to clean it. Until he disassembled and inspected it, he had no idea whether or not the gun would still function.

Luke gathered enough downed, dry mesquite branches for a small, almost smokeless fire. His flour had been ruined after being soaked in the Pecos, but his bacon and beans were salvageable, as was his Arbuckle's. He lit his fire, placed the frying pan and coffee pot on the coals, and soon had bacon and beans sizzling, his coffee boiling. Once the food was ready, Luke wolfishly gulped it down. Blaze also took several strips of bacon.

Once he finished eating, Luke scrubbed out his dishes and pans with sand. He then went to work on his weapons, taking apart both his six-gun and rifle. He cleaned and examined each part, oiled them carefully, then reassembled the guns.

"There," he said to Blaze, as he slid his Peacemaker back in its holster. "Now I can finally get some shuteye."

Luke's tobacco and cigarette papers had finally dried out. He rolled and lit a quirly, then stretched out on top of his blankets.

"Blaze," he said. "We've still got three days to go before we make Alpine, and another day after that to reach Marfa. I've already been shot at, beaten half to death, and nearly drowned. So far, the only good thing that's happened on this trip is me findin' you. I'm beginnin' to have my doubts I'll live long enough to even get anywhere near where we're headed."

Blaze whimpered. He licked Luke's hand.

"Yeah, you're right. There's no point in worryin' about things before they happen. Let's turn in."

Luke crushed out his smoke, pulled his hat over his face, and closed his eyes.

8

Despite Luke's trepidations, three days later, late in the afternoon, he reached Alpine without having any further trouble on the trail. Blaze's paws had healed well enough that he was now running alongside Luke's horses, only asking to be put in his carrier when he tired, or the ground was too rocky for the pup's still tender pads to handle.

"Wonder what's goin' on in this town, Pete," Luke said to his horse. As he rode down the main street, just about everyone stopped to watch him pass. The man they saw appeared to be merely a drifting young cowboy, perhaps one who rode the grub line, taking work at whatever ranch was hiring, then moving on, a man who never stayed in one place for long. Luke's nondescript clothing certainly caught no one's attention. After days on the trail, Luke's ruggedly handsome face was covered with a thick layer of dirt, and several days' stubble of whiskers. His black hair hung down over his ears and collar. The only things exceptional about his appearance were his deep blue eyes, which contrasted sharply with his black hair and thick, meticulously groomed moustache, and his height, since at a shade over six feet, Luke was taller than the average man.

Men or women who knew good horseflesh would also take note of his horses. While most cowboys disdained paints, or as many called them, particularly closer to Mexico, pintos, as Indian ponies, there was no denying Pete and RePete were exceptionally well built animals. Even after the long trip from Junction, despite the dried sweat and dust coating their hides, their gaunted appearance from lack of feed and water, they still moved smartly, lifting their hooves high, their eyes and ears alert. And of course their identical markings caught everyone's notice.

Little did the passersby know that, snugged inside Luke's vest pocket was his silver star in silver circle badge, a symbol of his authority. While most Rangers didn't wear a badge, Luke was one who did. It had been carved for him from a Mexican cinco peso coin by a Mexican silversmith in Del Rio.

"Folks seem damned unfriendly around here," Luke muttered under his breath, annoyed at the stares he was receiving. When two or three men gazed at him too intently, Luke glared back. The men quickly averted their gaze away from the stranger's piercing blue eyes. Something in them said this newcomer was not a man to be trifled with.

When riding into a new town, Luke would ordinarily stop first at the town marshal's or county sheriff's office, to introduce himself and let the local law know there was a Texas Ranger in the area. However, until he learned more about the territory, he decided not to reveal his identity to anyone. He rode past the building where both the Alpine Town Marshal's and Presidio County Deputy Sheriff's Offices were located. After stopping at a watering trough to allow Pete, RePete and Blaze to quench their thirst, he reined up in front of the first hotel he came to, the Alpine Haus. He dismounted and looped his horses' reins around the hitch rail. He gave each a lemon drop, and a pat on the neck.

"Wait here," he told them. "Soon as I get myself a room, I'll hunt up a livery stable. You'll get double rations of grain and extra hay tonight. C'mon, Blaze."

Luke's dog trotted alongside him as he went into the hotel's lobby. There was no clerk behind the desk, so Luke rang the bell sitting on the counter. A moment later, a middle-aged, balding man emerged from the room behind the desk. He looked Luke and his dog up and down.

"Good afternoon, sir. May I help you?" he asked, in a thick German accent.

"Howdy. I'd like a room for the night," Luke answered.

"Certainly. Just yourself?"

"And my dog."

"As long as he doesn't bark, your dog is welcome. The hotel does request that you not leave him alone in the room, when you go out."

"I wouldn't do that anyway," Luke answered.

"Excellent. You said just for tonight?"

"That's correct."

"The rate will be one dollar, which includes a pitcher of hot water, soap, and towels so you may bathe."

"That's a bit steep, but I reckon I can handle it for one night."

"Our establishment *is* more expensive than most frontier hostelries," the clerk admitted. "However, I'm certain you'll find that our lodgings are far cleaner, and much more comfortable, than anyplace else west of San Antonio."

"I can see that," Luke said, as he looked around at the lobby. Unlike the usually sparsely furnished, drab space that sufficed as lobbies in most Western small town hotels, the Alpine Haus's lobby was decorated with large oil paintings, most of scenes from the Swiss Alps. The chairs and sofas were covered in deep brown leather, the tables and desks made of ornately carved walnut or oak. Potted palms stood sentinel on either side of the front door. A large crystal chandelier illuminated the room.

"For some reason, the original owners of this hotel thought this dry, dusty region resembled their original home in Switzerland. They attempted to recreate a Swiss ambience, as best they could," the clerk explained. "Now that my family and I own the place, we've attempted to maintain the same atmosphere."

"I'd say they pretty much succeeded," Luke said. He chuckled. "They also must've been mighty homesick, to believe Texas looks anything like Switzerland."

"Indeed. Now, if you'll just sign the register, and pay for your room."

Luke signed the proffered book. He handed the clerk a silver dollar. The clerk took a key from one of the pigeonholes behind the desk. He handed it to Luke.

"Room 27. Top of the stairs then take a left. It's about halfway down the corridor, on the right. The room is opposite the street side, so it's a bit quieter."

"Tired as I am, an artillery battle wouldn't disturb me," Luke said, with a smile.

"I hope you have a pleasant stay, Mr. . . . Caldwell," the clerk said, looking at the register for his guest's name. "Is there anything else I may assist you with?"

"As a matter of fact, there is. The location of a good stable for my horses. And a recommendation of a place to eat. Also where I can cut some of the dust from my throat."

"We have an excellent dining room right here in the hotel. It opens for dinner at six. We also have a bier garten. The dining room features traditional German dishes, while the bier garten serves fine wines and lagers we import from Germany."

"That sounds good," Luke said. "How about the livery? I'm mighty particular about where I stable my animals."

"Francisco's Livery is a block down. He has an excellent reputation. Tell him Dieter from your hotel recommended his place."

"I'll do that," Luke said. "Danke."

"You know Deutsche?"

"You just heard every German word I know. Well, that and bier," Luke said.

He and the clerk both laughed.

"C'mon, Blaze. Let's go."

Luke went outside, and untied Pete and RePete. He led them the short distance to the stable. A young Mexican, probably still in his late teens, greeted them when they reached the livery.

"Hola, Senor. I am Francisco, owner of this stable. You wish stalls for your caballos?"

"Hola. Luke's my nombre. Si. Also, a good rubdown, and double rations for both, por favor. A good feeding in the mornin', also. I'll be leavin' about an hour after sunup. Dieter at the Alpine Haus told me you run the best stable in town."

"Dieter is correct. Tell him gracias for me. Your animals will receive the best care, senor. For an extra penny each, I will add some sorghum to their grain. Most caballos enjoy that."

"That'll be fine," Luke said. "Where can I stow my gear?"

"There is a room at the far end of the barn for saddles and other belongings. Your things will be safe there. My room is right across from it. I sleep with a shotgun. No one would dare try to steal any of the horses or belongings that have been entrusted to me. You have my assurance on that."

"Bueno. How much for the board?"

"Fifty centavos per caballo, plus the two centavos for the sorghum."

Luke dug in his pocket, pulled out a silver dollar, and handed it to the hostler.

"This should cover extra grain in the morning, too."

"Indeed it will, senor. Also sorghum. Gracias. Muchas gracias."

"Gracias to you, Francisco. Buenos noches."

"Buenos noches, Senor."

After returning to the hotel, Luke washed up, then took a nap before heading downstairs for supper. A buxom woman, who had graying blonde hair tied up in a bun, and light blue eyes, about the same age as the desk clerk, greeted him at the dining room's entrance. She reached down and patted Blaze's head. The pup wagged his tail.

"Ah, Mr. Caldwell. Guten abend. My name is

Helga. Lorelei will be your waitress. Bitte, this way."

She led Luke to an empty table by the front window.

"Is this satisfactory?"

"This'll do just fine. Danke."

"Excellent. Lorelei will be with you shortly."

"You lie down right next to me," Luke ordered Blaze, as he sat facing the window, so he could observe everyone coming and going. Blaze whined and wagged his tail. A moment later, a young woman, who was an exact image of what Helga would have looked like thirty years ago, came to Luke's table. Her blonde hair was also tied up in a bun, but hers was festooned with flowers interwoven. She wore a crisp white blouse, its bodice embroidered with flowers, and a full floral skirt. To Luke, her clothing appeared as if it were a traditional costume from her native land.

"Good evening, sir," she said, in lightly accented English. "I'm Lorelei. It will be my pleasure to wait on you this evening. I hope you're hungry. Our dinners are quite hearty."

"Good evenin', ma'am," Luke answered. "And yes, I'm plumb starved. Been ridin' for a few days now, and still have a ways to go. What's on the menu?"

"Tonight we have sauerbraten, which is beef in a tangy sauce, or wiener schnitzel, which is breaded veal. Those are accompanied with noodles, or boiled red potatoes if you prefer. The vegetable is boiled carrots. We also have sauerkraut."

"May I have some of all of 'em?" Luke asked. He smiled.

"Of course you may. We also have a very nice Liebfraumilch for your beverage, which I highly recommend. Or we have water, a stout German ale, or coffee."

"Liebfraumilch? What's that?" Luke questioned.

"A German white wine. It's not quite as dry as most white wines."

"I reckon I'll give that a try."

"I'm certain you won't be disappointed. For dessert, if you desire, we have apple strudel and coffee."

"Sounds good."

"I'll put your order right in. Oh, I nearly forgot. Would your dog like something? I can bring him a large bowl of meat scraps and trimmings. He certainly is a handsome boy."

Blaze, somehow knowing the young woman was speaking about him, looked up and whined. He wagged his tail expectantly.

"I think he'd appreciate that," Luke said.

"Wonderful. I'll bring those along with your meal, so he won't be pestering you by begging for some of your dinner. Would you like me to bring your wine now?"

"That will be fine," Luke said. "Thank you."

"It's my pleasure, sir," Lorelei said. She gave Luke a smile that would melt a block of ice.

"Meat scraps," Luke said to Blaze, once the waitress was gone. "Don't think you'll get spoiled like that by me."

Blaze lowered his head, covered his muzzle with his front paws, and gazed sadly at Luke with his soft brown eyes.

"Aw, hell!" Luke muttered.

Luke thoroughly enjoyed his meal at the Alpine Haus. It was a vast improvement over the usual small town café fare of beef or ham, slopped on a plate with lumpy gravy, soggy potatoes, and overcooked vegetables, which almost inevitably were beans, or black-eyed peas. As for comparing tonight's dinner to his own trail cooking of bacon, beans, and biscuits, sometimes supplemented by a rabbit or other small game he'd shot, Luke's stomach rumbled a protest at the very thought.

Much as he wanted to just turn in for the night, Luke needed information more. He stood on the sidewalk for a few minutes, smoking and taking in the cooler night air. At this altitude, over four thousand feet above sea level, the temperature dropped quickly once the sun went down. As soon as his cigarette was finished, Luke tossed the butt into the gutter, then crossed the street to the Chisos Saloon. He didn't really want any more liquor, having consumed the entire bottle of Liebfraumilch, but a saloon was always the best source of information in any small town.

"You'd better wait outside, boy," he told Blaze. "Just stay out of the way."

Blaze barked, and crawled under the boardwalk. Apparently, his experiences with the Jones family had taught him when, and where, to hide.

"Good boy. Stay there until I call you," Luke said. He pushed through the batwing doors and walked up to the bar. Conversation ebbed while the patrons looked over the newcomer, then resumed once Luke took his place between two groups of cowboys. Luke looked around the crowded barroom. Unlike many saloons, the Chisos appeared to be strictly a drinking establishment. There were no percentage girls in low cut gowns, no dance floor, and no derby-hatted piano player pounding the keys of an out of tune upright. There were no games of chance, only two card tables for anyone who might want to get up a card game. There was no professional gambler plying his trade in the place, either.

"Howdy, stranger," one of the barkeepers said. "What're you havin'?"

"Beer," Luke answered.

"Comin' right up."

The barkeeper filled a mug with the foamy brew, and set it in front of the Ranger.

"That'll be five cents."

Luke tossed a quarter on the bar.

"I plan on havin' more than one," he said, smiling.

"Sure. My name's Jake . . . Jake Caldicott. I own this place. Don't recollect seein' you in here before. You new in town?"

"Luke Caldwell. Yeah, I am."

"Stayin' a while? If I'm bein' too nosy, just say so."

"You're not . . . yet. I'm just spendin' the night. Only passin' through. I've gotta say, Alpine doesn't seem like the friendliest place I've ever visited."

"It used to be." Caldicott shrugged. "Mebbe, just mebbe, it will be again some day. Probably ain't gonna happen, though, until the owlhoots plaguin' these parts are cleaned out for good. Folks are plumb scared to death they'll be the next to get robbed, or worse."

"You're talkin' too damn much, Jake," one of the cowboys said. "You'd better keep your mouth shut. Otherwise, someone's liable to shoot it off for you."

"Just mind your business, Bobby Howell, and go back to your drinking," Caldicott answered. "I'm not gonna run scared. If we'd band together, we could stand up to those gangs."

"If we could even find 'em," Bobby retorted. "They hit real fast, then disappear into the brush before anyone can take their trail. Aw, the hell with it. Gimme another whiskey."

Caldicott splashed more red-eye into the cowboy's glass.

"What about the law?" Luke asked him. "I saw a deputy sheriff's office on my way into town. A marshal's office, too."

"Tom Skinner, he's the town marshal, tries his best, but he's only one man. The town won't even pay to hire him a deputy. And of course Skinner's jurisdiction ends at the edge of town. Hank Trammel, the deputy sheriff, is a good man, but he's runnin' himself ragged, goin' in circles tryin' to track down the renegades. We used to have two deputies, but Tim Sutton got himself ambushed about a month ago. Shot twice in the back, right in the middle of the street, in front of the bank. Whoever plugged him got clean away. Say, Luke, I don't suppose you'd be interested in takin' on the deputy sheriff's job? No one in town's been willing, not that I blame 'em."

Luke shook his head.

"Uh-uh. Not me. I'm a peaceable sort of feller, just moseyin' on down the trail, itchin' to see what's over the next hill."

"I reckon I can't blame you," Caldicott answered. "You'd probably just get yourself killed. Cleaning out the den of snakes in these parts is a job for the Texas Rangers. A whole troop of Rangers. But hell, that'll never happen. We've asked for 'em, but never get an answer.

Austin don't care about us, way out here. There's been talk of carvin' up Presidio County for some time now. It's way too large for one sheriff, who's at the county seat over to Marfa, to handle. No matter how many deputies he has. But that's all that ever happens, talk. Those politicians at the State Capitol are only interested in linin' their pockets, not helpin' decent, hard-workin' folks."

"More'n more folks are gettin' fed up," Bobby broke in. "There's quite a few who want to split West Texas off from the rest of the state. Make Alpine the new state capital. Then we can put together our own Rangers. Hell, I'd be the first one to sign up."

"I dunno," Luke said. "Seems to me that'd be bitin' off more than you folks can chew."

"We probably wouldn't be any worse off than we are now," Bobby answered, his voice bitter. "I had a small spread, just southwest of here, about ten miles out of town. It was in a little valley, with a spring that supplied enough water for a good sized herd of cows. I had a girl, too. Kathleen Davies. Was plannin' on asking her to marry me, once I got the ranch goin' good. Hell, I must've been plumb loco, thinkin' a gal like her could ever fall for a small rancher like me. Raiders hit my place one night, ran off all my stock, and burned down my cabin. Shot me and left me for dead. Only reason I'm still alive is I managed to crawl off into the brush. I guess they didn't want to take the time to look for me, and make certain I was done for. Those sons of bitches must've realized there was no way I could've identified 'em anyway. So I lost everythin'. The bank called in the mortgage, and Kathleen married Horace Moore, the bank president's son. Now I'm just a thirty a month and found horse wrangler at the Circle T. Gimme another whiskey, Jake."

"You sure you ain't had enough?"

"I reckon I'll know when I've had enough," Bobby answered.

"Suit yourself," Caldicott said. "But don't blame me if you wake up in a cell, with an awful bad headache."

He refilled Bobby's glass.

"I'm ready for another beer, too," Luke said.

"All right, Luke."

Caldicott took Luke's glass, refilled it, and placed it back in front of him. Luke took a large swallow of the amber liquid.

"Good beer," he said. "Bobby, did you ever think about takin' the deputy's job? It'd probably pay more than wranglin' horses, and would give you the chance to hunt down the hombres who destroyed your ranch."

"Hell, no. Them bastards damn near killed me once before. Never even got to pull my gun before they shot me down. I ain't gonna give 'em a second chance. There's way too many for a few men to handle. Like Jake said, we need a troop of Rangers. Or mebbe we start our own West Texas Rangers, rather'n waitin' for the big shots in Austin to get off their fat butts and do somethin'. When they were still roamin' around, the Comanches weren't half as bad as these hombres. Besides, I like horses. Workin' with 'em suits me just fine."

"Still, if enough . . ."

Luke's reply was cut off by a commotion outside, a dog's barking, then yelp, followed by a man's scream of pain. Blaze streaked under the batwing doors and ran behind Luke, where he stood, his tail between his legs, quivering and whimpering. Blood dripped from the pup's mouth.

"Blaze! What happened, boy?"

A burly man, bellowing in anger, burst through the doors. He was unkempt, his greasy black hair lank and uncut. His thick beard was tobacco stained, his buckskin clothing rank with sweat and dried blood. His dark brown eyes were set deep in their sockets. He had a bulbous nose, and heavy jowls, giving his face a rather hog like appearance. He held a skinning knife in his right hand. Blood dripped from where a large piece of flesh was missing from his left. His gaze settled on Blaze, who now was growling a warning, a low rumble deep in his throat.

"There's that mangy cur! Get outta my way, Mister. I'm gonna finish what I started."

He took two steps, before he stopped in his tracks. Luke had drawn his Colt. The big Peacemaker was pointed directly at the middle of the big man's substantial belly. The look in Luke's eyes made it clear he wouldn't hesitate to pull the trigger.

"Hold it right there," he ordered. "Unless you think you can digest lead. This here's my dog. If you touched one hair of his, you're a dead man. I can't possibly miss your big gut at this range."

"That damn dog ain't yours. It's a stray that was livin' on the streets. I was gonna kill it and skin it for its pelt. Sell the meat for pig feed. When I tried to grab him, he bit me. Now you aim to claim that mutt for yourself, so you can skin it. I ain't about to let that happen."

"My dog bit you? Hope he don't get poisoned from that."

The big man let forth a string of curse words.

"Curly, you get out of my place," Caldicott ordered. "You know you ain't welcome in here."

"I'm goin', soon as I take what belongs to me." To Luke he continued. "That gun you're holdin' don't scare me none. I can sink my knife in your belly before you even thumb back the hammer. Then I'll gut you *and* that damn dog."

"Is that so? Just hold on one minute. Don't do anything stupid. Bobby, if he does, plug him for me, will ya?"

"I've got him covered, Luke." Bobby had also

drawn his six-gun and had it aimed at Curly's ribs.

"Fine, Curly, I reckon we understand each other."

Luke slid his revolver back in its holster. He took his Bowie knife from the sheath on his belt.

Curly's lips opened in a broad smile, revealing crooked, tobacco-yellowed teeth.

"Now you're talkin' my game, you damned son of a bitch," he said. "I've killed plenty of men with this knife, not even countin' Indians and Mexicans. It's been too long since my blade's tasted blood. I figure after I gut you, I'll skin you and nail your hide up to dry."

"You gonna use that thing, or are you gonna talk me to death?"

With a roar, Curly charged at Luke, intending to overpower him and drive his knife deep into Luke's belly. Luke waited until Curly was almost on top of him, then sidestepped his rush. Curly's momentum carried him past Luke. His knife lodged into the front of the bar. Its blade jammed deep into the wood. Curly pulled it out, and swung back toward Luke, still off balance. Luke struck out with his own knife, its blade tearing through Curly's right wrist, the Bowie's heavy blade slicing through ligaments and tendons as if they were soft butter. Curly dropped his knife, his hand hanging uselessly. Luke slashed him across the belly. Curly backpedaled, eyes wide with fear. Luke struck again, slicing Curly's left cheek open from his ear to the corner of his mouth. Luke spun him around, and struck one final blow, which sliced across the back of Curly's left knee, separating the tendons and ligaments. Curly dropped to the floor, his blood soaking into the sawdust.

"You done killed me, you damn son of a bitch," Curly snarled, his hate-filled eyes fixed on Luke.

Luke wiped the blood off his knife on Curly's shirt, then replace it in its sheath.

"You ain't gonna die, long as someone'll stop the bleedin' enough for the doc to get here, and sew you up. But you ain't ever gonna knife another man or animal, not ever again. I made certain of that. You'll be a cripple for the rest of your useless life. I cut your face so you'll be marked for the rest of your days, just to make certain folks know who you are. Not that your stink doesn't let 'em know before you get within half a mile of 'em."

He hunkered on his haunches to pat Blaze's head.

"You all right, boy?"

Blaze barked, and licked Luke's face. The only injury Like could see was a small cut on the bottom of his dog's chin.

"Someone better go for the marshal, and the doctor," Luke ordered.

"Joe Malone's already on his way," Caldicott said. "He'll bring 'em both back."

"Good. I need a couple of towels."

"Here you go, Luke."

Caldicott tossed two unused towels to Luke.

"I'll clean up that cut, Blaze. You'll be just fine."

"Hey! I thought you wanted those to stop Curly's bleedin' out," Caldicott protested.

"I do. But my dog comes first."

Luke wiped the blood from Blaze's chin. The bleeding had already stopped. He stroked Blaze's head, then turned his attention to Curly. He had just tied one of the towels around Curly's right arm as a tourniquet, above his almost severed hand, when three men came rushing into the saloon. One was Joe Malone, who had brought back with him Alpine's Town Marshal, Tom Skinner, who carried a shotgun, and its only physician, Doctor Amos Pomeroy. Pomeroy hurried over to Curly, knelt alongside him, and opened his bag.

"How badly is this man wounded?" he asked Luke.

"I sliced him up pretty damn good," Luke said. "Right wrist's the worst. I just tied a tourniquet around it. You should be able to stitch him back together. Unless blood poisoning sets in, he should live."

"I'll have to take him to my office for surgery,"

Pomeroy said. "I'll need two men to carry him down there."

"My buckboard's outside, Doc," a man spoke up. "I'll haul him down there for you."

"That would be helpful," Pomeroy said.

"Jackson, Hollis, give Doc Pomeroy a hand gettin' Stokes to his office," Skinner ordered. To Luke he said, "I want your gun and knife. You've got some explaining to do. I've never seen you until just now, kneelin' alongside a man you admit you knifed."

Luke stood up and turned to face the marshal.

"I reckon I'll just keep my weapons," he replied, his voice calm and level. "I'll tell you exactly what occurred here tonight. My name's Luke Caldwell. I'm on my way to Marfa, and stopped here for the night. Got a room at the Alpine Haus, had supper, then dropped in here for a couple of beers. I left my dog outside. While I was havin' a last beer, I heard my dog yelp, then a man scream. My dog came runnin' inside. He hid behind me. Right behind him this son of a bitch, Curly I guess is his name."

"Yeah. Curly Stokes. Was a buffalo hunter, but with the herds mostly gone, he ekes out a living trappin' and huntin'. Keep talking."

"He told me he was fixin' to kill and skin my dog. I told him not to try it. He came at me with his knife. I could have killed him, but I didn't. Just made damn certain he'd never use a knife on

103

anyone, or any animal, ever again. I actually had my gun out, and could have shot him dead right where he stood. Don't ask me why, but instead I gave him a fightin' chance. Guess I figured a dose of his own medicine, and leavin' him a cripple, would be worse punishment than just shootin' him and bein' done with it. It was self-defense, Marshal, plain and simple."

"Anyone in here see it any different?" Skinner questioned. He was answered with a murmur of "nos" and shaking of heads.

"Things happened just like this hombre says, Marshal," Caldicott said. "You know I wouldn't allow Curly in my place, since he's always spoilin' for trouble. If anything, this man did the town a favor."

"Jake's speakin' the truth, Marshal," Bobby confirmed.

Skinner looked from Luke, to Caldicott, to Bobby, then back to Luke.

"I guess there's no use in me holdin' you for an investigation, Mister," he said to Jake. "You said you're only stayin' in Alpine for one night?"

"That's right. Then I'll be headin' on down the trail."

"Good. Make certain you're out of town before nine tomorrow morning. And keep that dog of yours under control. If not, I'll shoot him myself."

"Alpine'll be lookin' for a new marshal if you

do," Luke warned Skinner. "Because you'll be planted six feet underground, with a couple of my bullets in your belly. As far as my leavin', I'm planning on bein' gone well before nine. But if I wasn't, you can't order me out of town. I'm a Texan, and an American. That means I can go wherever I want to, and whenever I want. Perhaps, just perhaps, when my business in Marfa is finished, I'll stop back again. You have anything else you want to say?"

Skinner glared at Luke, then shook his head.

"I reckon not. Long as you're gone come morning."

"I've got no reason to stay," Luke retorted. "Since our business is concluded, I'm gonna have one more beer after all, then call it a night."

He turned his back on Skinner. The marshal stared at him for a moment, then cursed, turned, and stalked out of the saloon.

"Damn, Luke, that was somethin'," Caldicott commented, as he refilled Luke's mug. "I never would've believed any hombre could outduel Curly in a knife fight. And you said you're a peaceable feller. Boy howdy, I'd hate to think what you'd have done to Curly if you weren't."

"I *am* a peaceable hombre, sure enough," Luke answered. "Until I get riled. I just don't let anyone push me around. And no one touches my animals. If they do, they pay a high price."

"Seems as if," Caldicott said. He shrugged.

Luke thought for a few moments while he nursed his last beer. He came to a decision.

"Bobby," he said. "How tied down to the Circle T are you?"

"I've been there for a few months. Joe Dawkins is the head wrangler. You want the truth? He doesn't really need me. Oh, he and Lon Trenton, the ranch's owner, won't ever say so, but I know they put me on just 'cause they felt sorry for me. I didn't want anyone's pity, and I sure hate takin' charity from Lon, but I was out of money, and 'most starved to death. It was either take the job or die of hunger. I'm mighty grateful to Lon and Joe both, but if I had any other prospects, I'd most likely not turn 'em down, unless the job meant runnin' on the wrong side of the law. I'd never turn outlaw."

"You own a horse, or just the use of a string of ponies from the Circle T?"

"No, I've got a cayuse," Bobby answered. "A tough little mustang I caught and trained myself. Took me over a month just to catch him, then another three to tame him. I'd never give up Tony, not for all the gold in California. Even when I was down to my last nickel, Tony got fed."

"If you think you can leave the Circle T without any problems, I might have a proposition you'd be interested in. Tell you what. I can't talk in here. Grab your bottle and come back to my

106

hotel. We can palaver there. If you take on the job, fine. If not, all you've lost is some time."

Bobby shrugged.

"What've I got to lose? Let's go."

Bobby picked up his still quarter-full bottle.

"Jake, I'm gonna call it a night," he said. "Hasta la vista."

"That makes two of us," Luke added. "Good to meet you, Jake. G'night. C'mon, Blaze. Let's go."

"G'night, fellas," Caldicott replied. He turned his attention to another customer.

Luke and Bobby made the short walk to the Alpine Haus. They sat in two of the chairs on the boardwalk in front of the hotel. Blaze laid down next to Luke's chair. Bobby took a swallow from his whiskey bottle, then offered it to Luke.

"You want a swig of this?"

"Yeah, I reckon I could stand some," Luke answered. He took a slug from the bottle, then passed it back to Bobby.

"Nobody's around. I guess we can talk without bein' overheard," he said.

"I'm ready to listen to whatever you've got in mind," Bobby said. "There's nothin' holding me in this town."

"All right. But if you decide you ain't interested, this conversation never happened. Word can't get out to anyone, at least, not yet. Can I count on you to keep quiet, even when you've been drinking hard?"

"Hell, yeah," Bobby said. "I ain't a mean drunk, and I'm not one to shoot his mouth off, neither. In fact, I usually don't drink as much as I've had tonight. I was tryin' to drown my sorrows, but it didn't work. Whatever you've got to say won't ever be found out from me."

"Good. Because if it did, it could lead to me gettin' killed. You too, for that matter. Now that I've made that plain, are you still interested?"

"Let's say more like curious. You're kinda goin' around in circles, Luke. What the hell are you gonna ask me to get myself into?"

"I'm just being cautious, Bobby. That's what keeps me alive. Y'see, I'm not just a driftin' saddle tramp. I'm a lieutenant in the Texas Rangers. I'm here to clean out the renegades in this entire region. Stayin' incognito for the time bein'. From what I've seen already, I'm gonna need help. One thing a lawman learns real quick is to read people. I've gotten pretty good at it. Unless I miss my guess by a long shot, I've got a hunch you'll make a good partner. So, I'm offerin' you a job as a Texas Ranger. I'm not promisin' much. You'll only get paid thirty dollars a month, with the state providin' your ammunition, and nothing else. You won't even get your grub like you do workin' on a ranch. The state will provide you the funds to replace your horse, if it gets killed or crippled. Other than that, you get nada, except the chance of dyin' in a gunfight, from a knife in your guts, or an ambush bullet in your back. On the other hand, you'll know you're helping rid Texas of some muy malo hombres. With any luck, we might even track down the men who raided your ranch. So what do you say? I don't have time to let you think it over. I need an answer tonight."

"Lemme get this straight. You want me to quit a nice, easy job wrangling horses, with three squares a day, a clean bunk, and a roof over my head, and trade all that for one where the odds are I'll get killed."

"That pretty much sums it up." Luke paused, then laughed. "Oh, and you'll get to eat my trail cookin'."

"Somehow, that doesn't sound like you're addin' much to the pot, Luke."

"Trust me, once you sample my bacon and beans, you know it ain't addin' a damn thing. In fact, my cookin'll probably kill you faster'n any outlaw's bullet."

This time, Bobby laughed.

"Boy howdy, you really know how to convince a man, you know that, Luke?"

"I reckon. So what do you say?"

"I say you're plumb loco. But I must be too, because if you're willin' to take a chance on me, I reckon I can take one on you. I promise I'll do my best."

"Gracias. That's all I can ask."

"So, what do I need to do to get signed up?"

"Take the oath, and sign the enlistment papers. We won't do that tonight. I don't have the papers on me right now anyway. They're in my saddlebags up in my room. Plus, I don't want to chance anyone seein' us with the papers, and gettin' curious. So we'll do that after we hit the trail. The hard part, for you, is explaining to your boss why you're leavin' so sudden-like. Tell him anything you want, just don't let on that you're joining the Rangers. People say they won't talk, but you know word like that is bound to get out. I'm ridin' out just about an hour after sunup. I'll need you to meet me at Francisco's Stable then. How big a problem is that? I don't want your boss to get angry with you. It's never a good idea to burn your bridges."

Bobby shrugged.

"Quien sabe? I don't reckon it'll be a big one, though. Joe and Lon know I've been gettin' restless. I've been talkin' about movin' on for quite a spell now. Plus, like I said before, they don't really need me. They'll probably be relieved to have one less hand on the payroll. The Circle T owes me half a month's wages, but I'll let those go in exchange for leaving without warning. As far as packin' up, I don't own a lot of stuff. No more than I can fit in my saddlebags, or tie up in my bedroll. I'll head back to the ranch now. See you at Francisco's."

"If you do have any possibles, long as they ain't too heavy, bring 'em along. I have two horses. Use one as a saddle horse, the extra as a pack animal. Switch 'em off every other day. Keeps both of 'em fresher, so I can cover more ground."

"All right. I appreciate that. I do have a couple things I'd hate to leave behind."

"Most everyone does," Luke answered. "Hasta la vista, Ranger."

"Ranger. I kinda like the sound of that." Bobby grinned. "Texas Ranger Robert Josiah Howell. Won't that be somethin'?"

"We'll see if you still feel that way when the lead starts flyin'," Luke said. "C'mon, Blaze. Time to turn in."

9

Bobby was already waiting when Luke got to the livery stable the next morning.

"Buenos dias, Luke," he said. "Figured it wouldn't be a good idea to show up late for my first day of work."

"Buenos dias to you," Luke answered. "That's a right nice horse you've got there. He looks like he can handle a hard ride."

Bobby was holding the reins of a short-coupled mustang gelding. The horse was a chestnut, the color of old copper, lighter at the muzzle, with a flaxen mane and tail. He had white socks on all four legs. The mustang, as was characteristic of the breed, didn't stand too tall, probably a bit less than fifteen hands, but was powerfully built. He appeared to have plenty of stamina. Blaze walked up to him. The mustang lowered his head. He and Blaze sniffed each other's noses. Blaze licked the horse's muzzle. The mustang whickered softly in response.

Bobby ran his hand down his horse's sleek neck.

"Tony can go the distance, that's for damn certain. He's got plenty of bottom. Before he allowed me to be his pardner, he lived on nothin' but bunch grass and scrub brush. He don't need much feed and water. He's got plenty of speed, too. Aren't too many broncs who can outrun Tony. Ain't that right, boy?"

Tony muzzled his rider's shoulder.

"He and Blaze seem to have hit it off. That's a good sign," Luke said. "Speakin' of horses, I'd better get mine. You seen Francisco?"

"I am right here, Senor," Francisco said, walking out of the barn. "Your fine caballos have been fed, watered, and curried. They are ready for the saddle. Finer caballos I have never seen. In fact, I have never seen their equal, until this morning. Your amigo's caballo matches your animals, in grace, beauty, and power. I swear, by the Bendita Virgen Maria, Madre de Dios, and todos los santos en Cielo, especially San Francisco de Asis, I have been blessed by Dios Omnipotente this day." He made the Sign of the Cross. "Such beautiful caballos He has allowed my eyes to see. When I die, I hope He sends beautiful caballos such as these to carry my soul to Cielo."

"You want me to give you a hand saddling up, Luke?" Bobby asked. He indicated an oilskin wrapped bundle he held. "This contains the items I said I'd like to bring along. Tintypes of my family, and old jackknife my pa gave me. A cameo brooch my mother wore. A few other personal things."

"Sure. We'll get the packsaddle on RePete, then you can tuck 'em in with the supplies."

They went inside the barn. Pete and RePete nickered at Luke when they spotted him.

"Of course I've got your treats," he said. "Bought a whole sack of lemon drops for you two jugheads." He dug in his vest pocket, pulled out two candies, and gave one to each horse.

"That's all," he scolded, when they nuzzled his face, begging for more. "We've got a full day's ride ahead of us. If you both behave, I'll give you another treat later."

Bobby whistled in appreciation when he saw the twin paints.

"Dang, Luke, they're gorgeous. Never seen two horses that look identical before. I can't tell 'em apart. How'd you come to own 'em? They must've cost you a pretty penny."

"Actually, I got 'em for not much more than slaughter price," Luke answered. "They're twins, which are real rare, as I'm certain you know. That's why I named them Pete and RePete. The hombre who owned these boys didn't like paints, much like a lotta cowboys. He was gonna sell 'em for dog food. I saw their potential. He was too busy lookin' at their color. Kind of like someone judgin' a man by the color of his skin, rather'n what's inside him. He was glad to let me take the two off his hands. By the way, they aren't *quite* identical. Pete's got a small white spot under his chin. RePete's got one on the inside of his near hind leg. Other than that, you're right. There's no way to tell which is which, unless you look real close."

"Well, I'd say you got the better part of the deal," Bobby said. "They look like they can run."

"You'll find out before too long," Luke said. "I'll guarantee that. Let's get the saddles on 'em."

About four miles out of town, Luke turned his horses off the trail, and reined up near a large mesquite.

"What're we stoppin' for?" Bobby asked.

"Dismount. It's time to make you an official Texas Ranger. Wouldn't due to not have you sworn in all proper and legal before we run into any trouble."

"You figure we might have some before we reach Marfa?"

"I wouldn't bet my hat against it."

Luke and Bobby swung out of their saddles. After taking short drinks from their canteens, Luke administered the Texas Rangers oath to Bobby. He filled out two copies of the enlistment papers with a stub of pencil he carried in his vest pocket, using his saddle for a desk. Once Bobby signed them, Luke folded the papers, handed one copy to Bobby, and tucked the other into his saddlebags.

"Congratulations. I'll mail your papers as soon

as we get to Marfa," he said. "Make certain you hang on to your copy, until your official commission paper arrives from Austin. I'll have it sent to Alpine. I figure we'll be usin' it as our headquarters for the next month or so. The draft for your first month's pay should come back with your papers. If you need any money before then, I'll stake you to some."

"That shouldn't be necessary," Bobby said. "I've saved up some of my pay, so I'm flush. Long as I'm careful, I should have enough cash to see me through."

"Bueno," Luke said. "Let's get movin'. I want to get to Marfa before dark."

As they rode westward, the terrain became more rugged. The mostly flat to rolling, semi-arid high plains gave way to low mountains and mesas, the road winding through them. Some of the mountains were obviously the remnants of ancient volcanos. Almost all of them were good places for an ambush.

"Bobby, you mentioned you have pictures of your folks in that bundle," Luke said. "Are they still alive?"

Bobby shook his head.

"No. I lost my entire family due to dysentery, back in east Texas, close to the Gulf. I got it bad too, but I pulled through. That was about fourteen-fifteen years ago, I reckon. Since I was only sixteen, my uncle inherited the farm. Me'n him never did see eye to eye. Well, him and his two boys, my cousins. He'd work me like a dog, and my cousins would beat me up every chance they got. If my aunt tried to stand up for me, my uncle would slap her around. He was a drunk, too. That's one reason I try not to hit the bottle very often. Anyway, one day I'd had enough. When my cousins came at me, I whipped 'em both, real good. Beat the stuffin's out of 'em. I honestly don't know, to this day, who was more surprised, them or me. All I know is I left 'em both lyin' in the muck of the pig sty, and lit out. Never looked back. Headed west, got hired on as a horse wrangler at the Diamond M Bar outside San Angelo. I saved up enough money to buy a little place of my own. Then, the raiders hit, and took it all."

"Not quite," Luke said. "You're still here."

"Yeah, I reckon," Bobby conceded. "Ever since I lost my place, I've just been driftin'. Don't know what I would've done if Joe and Lon hadn't taken me on at the Circle T. Probably ended up a no-good drunk, just like my uncle." Bobby sighed. "Anyway, that's all in the past. Can't do anythin' about what happened that long ago. Mebbe signin' on with the Rangers'll give me the direction I've been lookin' for."

"Perhaps," Luke agreed. "But if you find out you're not cut out for law work, there'll be no hard feelings. We'll shake hands, say adios, and you'll be able to move on."

"All right. That makes sense. I appreciate you bein' honest with me."

"No reason I shouldn't be, is there?"

"No, I reckon not."

They rode in silence for a few minutes, then Bobby spoke up.

"You asked about my family, Luke. How about yours? You have one?"

"I sure do. My wife Addie, and four young'ns. Two boys and two girls. My home's in Junction. That's where I met Addie. I'd come home from a long stretch on the trail, and stopped by the town's newspaper to pick up a copy. Never expected to find a beautiful young woman running the paper. Addie had bought it from the previous owner, who wanted to retire. She'd come to Texas from back East, looking to make her own way in the world. A little bit like you are right now, as a matter of fact. I fell in love with her at first sight. I never figured a sophisticated lady from Philadelphia, Pennsylvania could fall in love with a fiddle-footed Texas Ranger. But I wouldn't give up. I was surprised it didn't take me as long to wear her down as I thought it would."

"Sounds like you've got a fine family," Bobby said. "Why the hell are you out here, riskin' your life every day, when you could be home with them? Settle down and become a town marshal, or county sheriff, if you want to stick with law work. Or mebbe start a ranch."

"I've asked myself that, more times than I can count," Luke answered. "Tried to once. But after a couple of weeks, I always have to be movin' again. Like I said, just plain fiddle-footed. I just have to see what's over the next hill. It was hard on Addie at first, but now we see eye to eye. She's a spunky lady. I hope when we're finished with our work here you'll get to meet her, and my kids."

"Yeah, I'd kinda like that."

Bobby grew silent, his gaze fixed straight ahead. Luke let him be, knowing the young man was facing a range of conflicting emotions. He just hoped one of them wasn't fear, an overpowering fear that could prove deadly in a gunfight with a band of desperadoes.

Luke studied his new recruit while they rode. Bobby was two years younger than Luke, as indicated by the date he'd provided for his enlistment records. He was about an inch shorter than Luke's just over six feet tall, but had a similar frame, broad through the shoulders, narrow at the hips, with a flat belly. His hair was blond, bleached almost to the color of straw where it wasn't protected by the flat-crowned dark gray Stetson he wore. His eyes were a light shade of blue. Like Luke, his skin was tanned a deep bronze by years of exposure to the harsh Texas sun and wind. Despite Bobby's attempts to keep his gaze looking straight ahead, to where the road reached the horizon, Luke noticed his eyes were constantly moving, taking in every detail of their surroundings. Bobby had a lime green bandanna tied loosely around his neck. He wore a dark red shirt, and faded denims, which were tucked into his scuffed black boots. He had a Smith and Wesson American .44 caliber revolver in the holster that rode high on his right hip. The gun was butt forward for a left-handed cross draw, a method which many men claimed was as fast, or faster, than the conventional draw. In a sheath hanging at his left hip was a bone-handled Bowie knife. There was nothing about him that would indicate he was more than a drifting cowboy. Except for their horses, which would catch the eyes of any man or woman who knew fine horseflesh, Luke was satisfied they would not attract much attention wherever they rode. Until he had a better handle on the situation in Presidio County, Luke hoped to keep people believing that, for as long as possible. He just hoped his instincts were right about the young man now siding him. If not, Luke's decision could prove fatal.

They rode for about another three miles, to where the road ran along the base of a slab sided mesa. The slight breeze which was blowing came from behind them. There was no sign of danger, no rabbits flushing from the brush, no flocks of birds disturbed from their perches bursting into flight, screeching in alarm. The horses, not even Luke's dog Blaze, indicated alarm at some hidden danger ahead. Even Luke, after years of law work his senses finely attuned to the least hint of trouble, was caught flat-footed when four horsemen emerged without warning from a jumble of fallen boulders at the base of the mesa's talus slope. All four held six-guns, which were pointed straight at Luke's and Bobby's chests. The Rangers pulled their horses to an abrupt halt. Blaze stood alongside RePete, his hackles raised.

"Stay quiet, boy," Luke warned his dog.

"Good afternoon, gents," the apparent leader of the outfit remarked. "Nice day, isn't it? A beautiful day for a friendly chat, wouldn't you both agree?"

"It is," Luke answered. "But those guns you've got pointed at us ain't exactly friendly."

"Our weapons?" the leader said. "You needn't worry about those. We intend you no harm."

"Now, why don't I believe you?" Luke answered.

"It doesn't really matter if you believe me or not. What happens next is your decision," the leader replied. "You men appear to be new to these parts. You may or may not be aware that various bandits and outlaw types have been plaguing this entire region. We just have to make certain you aren't lawbreakers, before allowing you to proceed."

"Are you duly authorized law officers?" Bobby asked.

"Not exactly, boy. Let's just say we're concerned citizens. We just intend to make certain anyone on this road isn't a troublemaker."

"That means they're vigilantes, pard," Luke said to Bobby, then continued to the group's leader. "I can assure you neither one of us is. We're just passin' through on our way to El Paso, then on to California. You've got nothing to worry about from us. We only want to reach the end of our trail."

"You just did," one of the other men said, with a guffaw.

"Now, Trent, don't be hasty," the leader scolded. "What my partner means is, to make certain you can't attempt any robberies, murders, or other such crimes, we must relieve you of your horses, weapons, and supplies. Everything but your canteens. After all, we would never leave a man stranded in this parched land without water. Once you do that, you'll be allowed to resume your journey, on foot. Without your boots, of course. We'll be taking those, too."

"Lemme get this straight," Luke said. "You're goin' to take everythin' we own, and leave us twenty some miles from the nearest town, with nothing but our canteens, which don't hold anywhere near enough water for us to reach civilization. Am I readin' you right?"

"You are indeed," the leader replied.

"Then you'll be signin' our death warrants," Luke retorted.

"Not necessarily," the leader disagreed. "You seem like an intelligent fellow. If you're resourceful, you will find a way to reach town. Admittedly, you won't have much of a chance, but you will have a slim one, nonetheless."

"And if we refuse?" Bobby asked.

"Then you'll die right here and now. These guns pointed at you aren't just for show. We mean business. You have ten seconds to make your decision."

Luke's deep blue eyes now held an angry glint. He glanced at Bobby, at the same time making a slight gesture with his right hand. He hoped that Bobby caught it, but not the outlaws. Whether Luke and his partner survived the next few minutes depended on it.

"Well, I guess we don't have much of a choice," he said.

"You don't have any choice," the man called Trent said, with a sneer.

"Let's not split hairs," Luke replied. "We'll do as you want."

He started to dismount. As he lifted his right leg over Pete's rump, he grabbed his Winchester from its sheath, raked his spur across Pete's rump, and dropped to the dirt. He rolled over twice, lay prone, and started firing. Pete ran straight into the middle of the men accosting the Rangers, sending two of their horses stumbling, off-balance. RePete and Blaze raced for cover.

Luke's first bullet ripped through the leader's stomach, came out his back, and clipped Trent's arm. His second and third bullets hit Trent in the chest, knocking him off his horse.

Bobby had rolled off Tony on the horse's right side, with his revolver in his left hand. His first shot took one of the men in the left side of his neck, severing the carotid artery. Blood spurted between the man's fingers as he gripped his throat, trying in vain to stop the flow. The last man, seeing his comrades down, was turning his horse to flee. Luke put a bullet into the man's left temple. At the same time, Bobby shifted his aim and shot him in the side. Bobby's bullet traveled through the man's abdomen, and lodged in a right rib. He toppled sideways off his horse, and lay quivering.

Luke got up, his smoking rifle still at the ready.

"You all right, Bobby?"

Bobby's voice was shaky.

"Yeah. I don't believe those hombres got off a shot."

"Let's check 'em. We can't chance one having

enough life left to put a slug in either of us before he dies."

Of the four men, only the leader was still breathing. He lay on his back, blood oozing from the bullet hole in his stomach. More blood seeped from between his lips. His six-gun was still clenched in his fist. Luke wrested it from his grasp and tossed it aside.

"You don't have much time, Mister," he said. "You want to give us your name, so we can let your kinfolks know? Your pardners' names, too."

"I'm . . . not . . . sayin' a word," the man gasped out, struggling to catch his last breaths. "Who the hell are you sons of . . . bitches?"

"Texas Rangers," Luke answered. "Legitimate law. Not like you."

The man's eyes widened. His body jerked and his muscles went into a spasm when a final jolt of pain shot through him. His face contorted in pain, then, with a final sigh, he exhaled his dying breath.

"He's gone," Luke said. He took a closer look at Bobby. His partner was trembling, and drenched with sweat.

"You sure you're all right? You look a little green around the gills. You didn't catch a bullet, or break somethin' jumpin' off your horse?"

Bobby shook his head.

"No. No, nothin' like that. I'll be fine in a couple of minutes."

"Wait a second!" Luke exclaimed. "You've never shot a man before, have you? *Have you?*" he repeated, louder, when Bobby hesitated.

"No, I damn sure haven't," Bobby admitted. "Got me feelin' kind of sick to my stomach."

"Why the hell didn't you tell me that when I asked you to become a Ranger?"

"You didn't ask me."

"Would you have admitted it if I had?"

"I dunno. Probably not," Bobby answered.

"Why in the blue blazes not?"

"Because I doubt you'd have signed me on if you knew I'd never shot anyone, let alone killed a man. Yeah, I've been shot, when those bastards raided my ranch, and I've seen men shot, some killed, but I've never shot a man myself, until today. Let alone killed one."

"It wasn't one. It was two," Luke pointed out.

"Mebbe one and a half," Bobby said. "We both got the last hombre."

He sucked in a deep breath, then gave a nervous laugh. "Can't say for certain my slug did much to that last son of a bitch. Your bullet caught him square in the head."

"Yeah, but yours might've hit him first," Luke said. "Either one would've killed him. Before we clean up here, I've gotta ask you, does this change your mind about bein' a Ranger?"

"Hell, no it doesn't. I'm feeling a bit better already."

"I hope so, because I'd hate to see you freeze up at just the wrong time," Luke stated.

"I won't."

"Good. I'm countin' on that. I've got to admit, you're handling killin' your first man far better'n I did. I puked my guts out."

Bobby laughed.

"We've been pushin' so hard there ain't nothing left in my belly to throw up," he shot back. He looked at the dead men. "What're we gonna do with these hombres?"

"We'll haul 'em into Marfa, and see if anybody recognizes them," Luke answered. "Here's hoping so. It'll be interesting to find out if they really were vigilantes, as they claimed, or just a bunch of outlaws masquerading as self appointed lawmen."

"I thought you wanted to keep our identities as Rangers unknown for as long as possible," Bobby reminded him. "Bringin' in four men draped belly down over their saddles is bound to attract attention."

"Ya really think so?" Luke said, with a grin.

"Well, mebbe just a bit."

"You're right, of course. But we have to tell the sheriff we're Rangers anyway. Just have to hope he keeps that knowledge under his hat. If not, we'll deal with it. It's a chance we've gotta take. These bodies might help lead us to some more renegades."

"Then let's load 'em up and get back on the trail," Bobby said. "Although I do have to wonder how they managed to lay in wait without us havin' any idea they were around. Tony almost always lets me know when there's somethin', or someone, prowling about."

"So do my horses," Luke answered. "But these hombres were well hidden. They kept their horses quiet, too. And with the wind at our backs, our animals, including Blaze, couldn't catch a whiff of their scent. Let's get to work. We'll wait until we get to town and let the sheriff search these bodies. We'll be with him, of course. But lettin' him do the searching should put his mind at ease that we're not gonna work without his help."

"That makes sense," Bobby agreed.

Pete had trotted back to Luke. RePete and Blaze emerged from their shelter to rejoin their companions. Tony was with them.

"You fellas all right?" Luke asked. He checked Pete's rump, to make certain his spurs hadn't gouged the big gelding's hide. The only damage was some lost hair, scraped off by the spurs' dull rowels.

"I'm sorry I had to do that to you, pal," Luke apologized to the paint. "You did real good, scattering those devils. I've got a treat for you. You boys also. And one for your horse, Tony."

Luke dug in his saddlebags and removed a stale biscuit. He broke it into four pieces, giving one to

Bobby. He tossed one piece to Blaze, then gave the remaining pieces to his horses. He looked up at the sun.

"We should still reach Marfa with plenty of daylight left, unless we run into more trouble, Bobby."

"From what you've told me about the trouble you've already had, I sure ain't countin' on that," Bobby said.

"I reckon I can't blame you. Let's get these bodies on their horses. They sure as hell ain't gonna climb up there by themselves."

"If they do, you'll be on your own. I'll quit right here," Bobby said. "I'll be halfway back to Alpine before you can say two words. And that's usin' my own two feet, not even my horse."

"If they do, I'll be right behind you," Luke said.

An errant gust blew Trent's hat off. It ruffled his shirt and hair.

"Damn, if he don't look like he's comin' back from Hell," Bobby said. "You can handle that one, Luke. I'll take one of the others."

The four dead men were draped over their horses, the bodies lashed in place. Their guns were recovered, and placed in Luke's packsaddle. When Luke and Bobby resumed their journey, the only signs of their gunfight with the vigilantes were blood darkened dirt, and a jumble of hoof prints.

10

It was late afternoon when Luke and Bobby rode into Marfa. They looked straight ahead, ignoring the stares of people on the boardwalks. They ignored questions shouted from the crowd which gathered and followed them to the Presidio County Sheriff's Office. Having heard the commotion, Sheriff Wilbur Clayton, along with one of his deputies, was standing on the boardwalk in front of his office when the Rangers reined in, turned their horses to the hitch rail, and dismounted. Clayton looked at the pair, then the four horses they led, carrying their grisly burdens.

"Who the devil are you hombres? What's the meaning of this, totin' a bunch of corpses into my town? Don't try tellin' me you just happened to stumble across those hombres!"

Blaze had gotten too tired to continue walking, so he was in his carrier, which was attached to Luke's packsaddle. Luke untied the carrier and set Blaze on the ground, then went to the string of horses tied to RePete's packsaddle. He began loosening the first horse's lead rope.

"Did you hear me, Stranger?" the sheriff yelled.

"I did," Luke answered. "I'm not deaf. Soon as I get these horses settled we can palaver. And no, we sure didn't just stumble across these hombres. We killed 'em."

"You done what?" the deputy shouted.

"Keep still, Matt. Let me handle this," the sheriff said. To Luke he continued, "Did I hear you right? *You* killed these men?"

"Well, not by myself, and not because we wanted to," Luke answered. "My pardner also took a hand. They didn't give us a choice. It was us or them. And it for damn certain wasn't gonna be us."

"You'd better have a damn good explanation,"

"I'd say the fact they tried to drygulch us is a pretty good one," Luke answered, still untying the horse, then leading it to the hitch rail. "About twelve miles east of town. Claimed they were vigilantes, makin' certain we weren't outlaws riding into the territory. They told us they intended to take everything we owned, except our canteens, and leave us afoot. Me'n my pard took objection to that. Since they were gonna fill our briskets full of lead when we told 'em no, pumpin' them full of slugs instead seemed like the thing to do, at the time. We could have just left 'em out there in the malpais for the buzzards and coyotes. No one would've been the wiser, and it would have saved us a whole lot of trouble. But we brought 'em in to turn them over to you, and see if you, or anyone in Marfa, might know who they are. You mind taking a look? I'm more than a mite curious as to whether or not they are townsfolks, who decided to take the law into their own hands. The hombre on the buckskin was the leader of the outfit. He called the one lyin' across the bay 'Trent.' "

"Trent?" the sheriff repeated.

"Yeah, Trent," Luke confirmed.

"Hell! That's gotta be Trent Lonergan," the deputy exclaimed.

"Don't go jumpin' to conclusions, until we take a look," the sheriff said. He walked over to the buckskin, and lifted the dead man's head by its hair. He uttered a curse, and let the man's head fall back.

"It's Lake Connolly. That means Trent Lonergan *is* one of the others. Let's see who the rest are."

He checked the other three men, confirming Lonergan's identity. The remaining two were Jorge Alvarado and Lake Hawkins. A murmur ran through the crowd as they recognized the dead men.

"You claim these men tried to rob and kill you?" Clayton asked.

"Yes," Luke answered.

"They damn sure did," Bobby added.

"I'm havin' trouble believing your tale," Clayton said. "You certain you don't want to change it?"

"Not one word," Luke snapped. "Why would I want to? Who exactly are these men?"

"Lake Connolly ran the biggest gambling parlor in Marfa. The other three worked for him as dealers. So, knowing that, tell me one reason why they'd be out tryin' to rob folks? Especially in broad daylight."

"Probably pulled their holdups durin' the day when everybody figured they were either sleeping, or just out for a ride, since gambling houses open late and close early?" Bobby said.

"I wasn't talkin' to you," Clayton retorted. To Luke he said, "I'm waitin' for an answer."

"Beats me," Luke answered, with a shrug. "Why don't you ask them?"

The sheriff's face flushed deep red, almost purple with rage.

"Because they're dead, ya danged idjit. I ain't buyin' that windy you're tellin', neither."

Behind Luke, Bobby's voice was low and deadly, as he issued a warning.

"Uh-uh. I wouldn't try that if I were you. Unless you're fixin' to be planted in the graveyard, along with these other fellers."

Clayton's deputy had started to pull his gun. He froze, with his hand just over the butt of the revolver. Bobby had already pulled his own pistol and had it pointed straight at the deputy's belly.

"I don't give a damn whether you believe me or not, Sheriff," Luke said. "Now we can either go inside your office, and talk reasonably in private, or we can have a bloodbath, right here in the street."

"You're outnumbered," Clayton sputtered.

"That don't matter none, at least for you. Because you and your deputy will take the first bullets. Dead men don't much care about who won the argument. What's it gonna be?"

Clayton swallowed hard. The glint in Luke's deep blue eyes told him this newcomer meant exactly what he said. If any shooting started, Clayton and his deputy wouldn't live through it.

"I reckon we can palaver in private," he said. "Matt, get those bodies down to Fred Keane. He'll need to get busy building coffins. The rest of you, break it up. There's nothing more to see here. Go on about your business."

"You might want to have your deputy tell the undertaker not to do anything with the bodies until you can examine them, Sheriff," Luke said. "We don't want him goin' through their pockets, and removing anythin' that might be evidence."

"You're right, Mister. Matt, tell Keane not to do anything with those corpses except lay 'em out, until I get there. You stay with 'em and make certain no one touches 'em until I say so."

"I'll make certain of it, Will."

"See that you do. You two, c'mon inside."

"Blaze, you stay here," Luke told his dog. "I'll be back soon as I can."

Blaze whined, then curled up alongside Pete.

Luke and Bobby followed the sheriff into his office, which consisted of one room with two desks, and an annex with a bank of four cells. Clayton sat behind the right hand desk. He waved Luke and Bobby to ladder-backed chairs against the opposite wall.

"Smoke if you want," he said, as he pulled a pipe out from his vest pocket. He filled it with tobacco from a jar on his desk, tamped it down, struck a match to life on his boot sole and touched the flame to the pipe, inhaling deeply until the tobacco took hold. Luke and Bobby rolled and lit quirlies. While he built his cigarette, Luke studied the county lawman. Clayton was only a few years older than the two Rangers. He was about average height and weight, with brown hair and eyes. It was too soon for Luke to be certain, but from first appearances, Clayton looked to be a competent lawman. He took a form from his top desk drawer, along with a pencil.

"Now," Clayton began. "I've got a hunch there's more to this story than you men are letting on. First of all, you mind givin' me your names, for the record."

"My handle's Luke Caldwell, my pardner's is Bobby Howell. You must be Wilbur Clayton, the county sheriff. We were on our way to see you."

"I am," Clayton confirmed. "What business do you have in Marfa, with me in particular?"

Luke reached into his vest pocket and took out his silver star on silver circle badge.

"We're Texas Rangers. I'm a lieutenant in the outfit. Bobby's a new recruit. We were ordered here in response to complaints about extensive outlaw activity in Presidio County. The ambush we rode into pretty much confirms the reports Austin's received are right on the money. Now, before we talk further, I'd rather it not be known we're Rangers, at least not right off."

"Anybody can show a badge," Clayton said.

Luke sighed.

"Show the man your commission papers, Bobby."

Luke took out his billfold, and removed his commission from his wallet. Bobby passed his papers to Luke, who handed both sets to the sheriff.

"Satisfied now?" Luke asked.

"These seem in order," Clayton admitted. He handed the papers back to Luke. "I'm puzzled as to why you're here, though. I didn't send for any help from the Texas Rangers."

"I didn't say you had," Luke answered. "Exactly how bad is the outlaw situation in this county?"

"Well, it ain't good, I'll concede that. But it's nothing me and my deputies can't handle."

"Not according to the complaints Austin's received," Luke said. "If those are correct, the

136

renegades pretty much have free rein in parts of Presidio. The northern half of the county, in particular, seems to be overrun with killers, thieves, and rustlers."

"Hell, it ain't my fault if the county is too damn big for my office to cover all of it right," Clayton protested. "If the county judges won't give me the money to hire enough deputies, what do they expect's gonna happen?"

"I can understand your frustrations," Luke empathized, "but that still doesn't solve the problem. That's why we're here, to lend a hand cleanin' out the skunks."

"Me'n my men have been doin' all right," Clayton said. "If the politicians would get off their sorry butts and break off parts of Presidio into new, smaller counties, like they've been yappin' about for years, then we wouldn't be having this conversation. You must know what I mean. The Rangers have been undermanned for years. Most law enforcement organizations are."

"I do, but that's not your problem," Luke answered. "The outlaws running roughshod over half of the county are."

"Would you mind tellin' me who wrote Austin?" Clayton asked.

"As a matter of fact, yes. That information's confidential. I can tell you it was more than one individual. Several more."

"I've got a good idea who some of them are anyway," Clayton muttered.

"Sheriff, I hate to be blunt, but we're wastin' time here. Me'n my partner have had a long, hot, dusty ride. Our horses are worn out, too. We need haircuts, shaves, and hot baths, a good meal, and a hotel room. Our horses are more'n ready for a good feedin', grooming, and stall rest. They need new shoes, too. I've got just one question. Are you willing to cooperate with us, and work together, or are we gonna be on our own?"

"I'll help you as much as I can," Clayton grudgingly answered. "But don't expect a lot. I don't know much more about those renegades than you do. I'll give you what information I can."

"Bueno. We're obliged," Luke said. "Since I don't want it known we're Rangers, at least for a while, I'll leave gatherin' evidence from Connolly and his men's bodies to you. You might want to search his gambling parlor, too. If he and his men were robbin' folks, there's probably a stash of stolen goods hidden somewhere on his property."

"I'd have to get a warrant," Clayton pointed out.

"Not necessarily. Connolly's dead, so he sure as hell won't complain you didn't obtain one. If you'd feel better having a warrant, and I don't blame you for that, I'm certain a county judge

138

will have no problem issuing one. Me'n Bobby will testify about what happened, if you need us for that. Any other questions, or objections?"

"I reckon not," Clayton said.

"Good. Let's get the report on this ambush done, so me and Bobby can get cleaned up, eat, and turn in for the night. What's a good, inexpensive hotel?"

"The Marfa Manor. It's not fancy, but it's clean, and quiet."

"That's all we want," Luke said. "We'll spend the next two nights there. After that, we'll head on out, and start roundin' us up some desperadoes. If you could get us a list of where they seem to be thickest, and how many you think we might be up against, that would be helpful."

"I'll do that," Clayton agreed. "I was gonna ask you to stick around town for a couple of days anyway, until the coroner completes his report. You might have to testify at a coroner's inquest."

"That won't be a problem," Luke said. "You'll know where to find us. Now, let's get at that report."

Luke and Bobby's first stop after leaving the sheriff's office was the Marfa Livery Stable, where they left their horses in the competent care of a young Black hostler, who assured them Pete, RePete, and Tony would receive a good rubdown, along with full buckets of grain and plenty of hay.

"Now that our horses are settled, it's time to get ourselves curried," Luke said, as they walked away from the stable, rifles in hand and saddlebags slung over their shoulders. "First we'll hunt us up the hotel and get a room. Soon as that's done, we'll find the barber. I'm lookin' forward to a nice, long soak in a tub full of steaming hot water."

Much to their chagrin, the barber had closed his shop early for the day, so Luke and Bobby had to settle for washing up as best they could in their hotel room. They ate supper at a nearby restaurant. Rather than following their meal with a visit to the closest saloon, they decided to turn in early for the night. As luck would have it, the only room the Marfa Manor had available held two full sized beds. Luke was able to talk the proprietor into letting them have the room for the same price as a single.

The lamp had been turned low, the flame just high enough to keep the room from complete darkness. Luke was stretched out on his belly in his bed. Bobby was lying on his back, staring at the ceiling.

"Luke?"

"Yeah, Bobby?"

"That sheriff knows more than he's lettin' on."

"You really think so?"

"I damn for certain do."

"Why?"

"I can't quite put my finger on it. Just a gut feelin', I guess. I'm not saying he's involved with the outlaw gangs, leastwise not yet. But there was something in his eyes. He didn't seem to look straight at us while we were talking. He kind of hesitated when answerin' your questions, too. I dunno. Hell, mebbe I'm all wrong."

"No. You're not wrong. I'm not certain what Sheriff Wilbur Clayton is hiding, but he was definitely holdin' something back. It might not be anything, perhaps he's just got a bad case of professional jealousy. Quite a few local lawmen don't like to see Rangers come in and usurp their authority. Or, it just could be he's in cahoots with some of the gangs. We'll just have to see what we can turn up."

"And keep our eyes open, just in case the good sheriff decides to put bullets in our backs. I'd wager he'd do a better job of drygulchin' us than those hombres that tried it this afternoon."

"Now you're talkin' like a lawman. You're learning fast, pard. And I sure wouldn't take that bet. Clayton knows every nook and cranny of this town. Probably most of the county, too. You can be certain if he decided to bushwhack us, I'd bet my hat we'd never know until it was too late. We might've walked plumb into a hornets' nest. We could have to take on the owlhoots, and the local law. Which means we've got to be alert, and that means rest. Go to sleep. Bobby. Good night."

"G'night, Luke."

Luke and Bobby spent the next day taking care of chores. They brought their horses to the blacksmith to have their feet trimmed and shoes replaced. After that, they went to Harold's Tonsorial Parlor, where they got badly needed haircuts, shaves, and baths. Harold, the barber, also caught them up on much of the local gossip. In any small town, next to the saloon, the barber shop was the best place to pick up tidbits of information.

Luke wrote up a report of what had happened on his assignment so far. He took that, along with Bobby's enlistment papers, to the Wells Fargo stage depot, to put in the outgoing mail for the next eastbound stage. After that, the Rangers went to the Western Union office, where Luke sent a brief message that he had arrived, adding that he had recruited a new man into the Rangers. They spent the rest of the afternoon strolling around Marfa, stopping at the Marfa Mercantile to pick up supplies, and familiarizing themselves with the town's layout. With nothing to do until supper, they returned to their hotel for a nap. They had supper in the hotel dining room. After that, they decided to visit a local saloon, to have some beers and see if they could find more information on the outlaws plaguing Presidio County.

Luke and Bobby were halfway across the street when a man emerged from the Presidio Cantina. He stopped dead in his tracks, staring at Luke in recognition.

"Luke Caldwell," he screamed. "I've been waitin' years for the chance to get even with you. I've been lookin' for you ever since I got released from Huntsville. And, damn, there you are, standin' right in front of me, big as life, without a care in the world. Well, Caldwell, that's all about to change. I'm gonna kill you. Drop you in your tracks, right where you're standing. You understand me?"

"Errol Milan, of all the rotten luck," Luke answered, his voice steady. "How the devil did you get out of Huntsville?"

"I got parole. Time off for good behavior. Ain't that somethin'?"

"Whoever granted you parole must've been plumb out of their mind, Milan. I reckon you've probably robbed a few more banks since you got out."

"Don't matter to you what I've done, or haven't done. All that matters is you're gonna die tonight. That your dog?"

Blaze was standing against Luke's left leg, growling.

"He is."

"Then I'm gonna kill him too."

Bystanders scattered for cover. Two cowboys untied their horses and led them down the street, away from any errant bullets.

"Bobby, stand aside," Luke ordered. "This is personal. But if this low-down, back-shootin' son of a bitch does somehow manage to plug me, kill him. And take care of Blaze for me."

"Sure thing, Luke."

Bobby edged about seven feet from Luke's side. His left hand hovered over the gun hanging at his right hip, ready for a cross draw.

"We've jabbered long enough," Milan snarled. "You ready?"

"Whenever you are."

Both men grabbed for their guns. Luke's hand stabbed downward, then lifted his Peacemaker from its holster in a blur. Milan had just cleared leather when Luke fired. His bullet took Milan in the belly, two inches above Milan's trousers' waistband. Milan staggered back into the cantina's wall, his left hand clamped to his bullet torn gut. He attempted to aim his gun, but his strength was rapidly failing. Milan only got off one shot, which plowed into the dirt at his feet. He bounced off the wall, and jackknifed into the street, twisting as he fell to land on his back. Luke kept his still smoking gun aimed at the downed man. Bobby had also drawn his six-gun, holding it leveled at Milan. Milan shuddered, coughed up blood, and went slack. Blaze walked over to the dead man, sniffed at him, lifted his right hind leg, and peed on Milan's face.

"Blaze. Get back here," Luke called. The dog barked, and ran back to him, his tail wagging.

"Bad dog," Luke scolded, while laughing at the same time. "We don't want that hombre to be comin' around. Don't you be tryin' to rouse him."

Luke and Bobby walked up to Milan's body. He was indeed already dead, unusual for a belly wound. The amount of blood soaking his shirtfront and filling Milan's mouth indicated Luke's bullet must have severed a major artery, or perhaps struck a rib and deflected into his heart, possibly severing the aorta on its path. Luke punched the empty shell casing from his Colt's cylinder and replaced it with a fresh bullet.

Most of the people who had taken shelter during the brief fight emerged from their hiding places. They gathered around the body lying in the street, the crowd, like always, morbidly fascinated by sudden, violent death. Their numbers were supplemented by customers of the saloons, brothels, and gambling parlors who came out to see what had occurred. An extremely skinny, tow headed young man, wearing a town marshal's badge on his roughout cowhide vest and carrying a rifle, pushed his way through the mob. He glanced at Milan's body, then looked at Luke and Bobby, who still held their guns.

"Marshal George Norton. Would one of you gentlemen explain what just happened here?"

"Sure, Marshal," Luke said. "The dead hombre is Errol Milan. He's got a record as long as your arm. We had a run-in quite some time back. I caught him red-handed stealin' a herd of my horses. I should have shot the bastard on the spot, but I turned him over to the law. He was sentenced to ten years in Huntsville. He swore he'd get even with me one day. I didn't realize he'd been released, let alone was here in Marfa. He came out of the cantina and spotted me. He said he'd been lookin' for me ever since he got out from behind bars. Told me he was gonna kill me, as he'd promised himself. There was no way I was goin' to be able to talk him out of it. When he went for his gun, I had to pull mine. I was quicker. It was self-defense."

"Ain't you and your compadre the hombres Sheriff Clayton told me rode into town today, leadin' a string of horses carryin' dead bodies?"

"That'd be correct," Luke answered.

"Seems to me there's been a lot of sudden deaths from gunshots since you hombres showed up here. As I recollect, the sheriff told me you claimed the men you brought in also tried to steal your horses."

"They did," Luke said.

"And everything else we own," Bobby added.

"Were the horses he tried to steal from

146

you before also pintos?" Norton asked Luke.

"Yeah, as a matter of fact they were," Luke answered. "What difference would that make? Don't mean a thing. A horse thief is a horse thief, plain and simple."

"I saw your horses in the livery stable, cowboy," Norton said to Luke. "I'm havin' a hard time believing anyone would want those crowbaits, except mebbe a lousy Indian. No self-respecting white man would ride a damn pinto. Unless this Milan hombre intended to sell your horses for dog food."

"Marshal, unless you've ridden hard for over three hundred miles chasin' someone across the desert, I'd advise you to keep your mouth shut about another man's horses," Luke snapped, struggling to keep his temper in check. Anyone who criticized Luke's horses often ended up with a punch in the mouth. "I'll put my broncs up against any other horse in this state. What color my horses are has nothin' to do with what happened tonight. Kinda like the color of a man's skin doesn't matter, it's what's inside his skin that counts. Let's get back to the business at hand. Milan tried to kill me. I shot him before he could. Me'n my pardner'll give you a statement tonight, or first thing in the mornin'. The coroner ruled that our killing the men who ambushed us was justified homicide, so our business here in Marfa is done. We'll be movin' on tomorrow. Let's get this matter settled before then."

Norton glared at Luke, then turned his attention to the crowd.

"Anyone here see what happened? Is this hombre tellin' the truth?"

"I saw everything, Marshal," one of the spectators said. "I was just closing up my shop. That dead hombre came out of the cantina, and told this other man he was gonna shoot him down where he stood. He drew first. This man was lots quicker. He plugged the other one dead center, before he could even pull the trigger. It was a clear case of self-defense."

"Thanks, Harvey. You'd be willing to sign a statement to that effect?"

"I would, Marshal."

"So would I, Marshal," one of the women from the cantina said. "The dead man tried to get rough with me. Pablo had to take out his shotgun, and order him to leave. I was watching him from the window, to make certain he wasn't coming back. As soon as he saw this man, he screamed that he'd been looking for him, and that he was going to kill him. I was happy to see him get killed. He was el puerco."

The woman spat on Milan's body.

"Gracias, Lola," Norton said. To Luke and Bobby he continued, "I reckon things happened the way you say. You're both free to go. I'd just request you come by my office to sign statements. We can do that now, if that's preferable."

"We'd rather get it over with," Luke said. "I reckon we'll forget about havin' some drinks tonight. We'll make out our statements, then go back to our hotel and turn in."

"Fine. Two of you men, take the body down to Keane's. He's been having a profitable couple of days." He looked at Luke and Bobby, then gave a short laugh. "He'll probably be sorry to see you boys leave town. He'll most likely be the only man in town who'll feel that way. As far as the rest of Marfa, good riddance."

"I said we'll be movin' on come tomorrow, Marshal," Luke replied, with a thin smile. "I never said we wouldn't be comin' back."

11

Luke and Bobby rode about twenty miles the next day. Luke chose a campsite at the back of a slot canyon, which wound far back into a slab sided mesa. As they rode deeper into the narrowing canyon, Bobby looked up nervously at the beetling cliffs looming overhead. The canyon walls were so close together their horses were now walking in the babbling waters of a shallow brook which issued from its depths. Its bed filled the canyon floor from wall to wall. Dusk had already enveloped the canyon's depths, the sun's rays blotted out by its steep sides.

"Are you certain this damn place is safe, Luke?" Bobby asked. "Seems to me a piece of those cliffs could come tumblin' down at any time."

"It's a helluva lot safer than spendin' the night out in the open," Luke answered. "There's still a few bands of renegade Mescaleros roamin' around these parts."

"Apaches?"

"Yup. Even old Victorio himself still raids around this territory. We don't want to come across any of them if we can help it."

"You reckon there's any about right now? And if there are, do you think they know we're here?"

"Quien sabe?" Luke said. "They could be within two feet of us and we'd never know it. One thing for certain, if there are any Mescaleros prowlin' around, they know we're here. You can bet your hat on that. And your scalp."

"That's not funny, Luke."

"I wasn't making a joke. That's why we're gonna spend the night in this canyon. If any renegades, no matter what color they are, decided to attack us, we'll be able to defend ourselves. We can have a fire, too. The walls will keep the smoke in, and its scent from driftin' to any intruder's nose. We'll be able to keep the horses close, too. I don't need to tell you what'd happen to us if an Apache stole our mounts, even if he didn't bother to kill us."

"Are the Indians as cunning as I've heard tell?" Bobby asked.

"Pretty much. Don't forget this was their land for hundreds of years, before us Whites starting pushing them out. They know every square inch of this land, where waterholes are located that no White man would ever find. I can't hardly blame them for fightin' so hard to keep what was theirs. The Apaches were pushed down this far when the Sioux forced the Comanches out of the plains, so the Comanch' drove the Apaches out of their former hunting grounds. The Apaches aren't as good fighters on horseback as the Comanch', but they're good enough. Plus, an Apache can travel for days on foot, with hardly any food or water. An Apache brave can even outrun a man on horseback, over a distance. He can keep on goin', when the horseback rider has to stop and rest his mount. I've fought both the Comanche and the Apache, along with the Kiowa. They're all damned good fightin' men. The only reason us Whites have been able to force them out is the diseases we give them, and the fact we outnumber 'em. The Indians are fightin' a losin' battle, and they know it. But the way they live is the only way they've ever known. Most of 'em'll never adopt the White man's ways."

"You kind of feel sorry for the Indians, don't you, Luke?"

"Yeah, I do. Most of the Mexicans, too. Even though most of the Mexes we come across were born right here in Texas, and are citizens of the state, and the country, lots of Whites would like to eradicate them, along with the Indians. Hell, mebbe some day we can all live together, and in peace. Until then, our job is to fight the outlaws, and make Texas safe for honest folks. Shoot, I must sound like some damn idealist. It's never gonna happen."

"Probably not in our lifetimes, but it'll happen. God wouldn't have it any other way. It's just gotta wait until the Devil and his minions stop tusslin' with the good folks, and God's angels."

"I like your thinkin', Bobby," Luke said. "This

canyon's starting to widen a bit. I can see the headwall just ahead. We'll be making camp in a few minutes."

Luke and Bobby had made camp, cared for their horses, and eaten supper. They were seated cross-legged alongside the dying fire, having last cups of coffee and cigarettes.

"Bobby, I've got somethin' I've been meaning to tell you," Luke said. "I guess now's as good a time as any."

"What is it, Luke?"

"I know you'd never killed a man until the other day. I also know it wasn't easy on you. Just listen to me," Luke said, when Bobby started to protest. "First, every time you get into a gunfight, you'd better be scared . . . damn scared. Any man who says he isn't is either a liar, or a fool. A man who isn't afraid when the bullets are flyin' gets reckless. He makes mistakes, and sooner or later, that gets him killed. The other thing is never let having to kill a man stop bothering you. Hell, I've been a lawman for years, and I still hate havin' to gun a man down. If you feel nothing when you shoot a man, or even worse, start to enjoy it, that makes you no better than the outlaws we're facin'. You understand what I'm tryin' to tell you?"

"Yeah, I do, Luke. But that was two things."

"I guess it was, at that," Luke said, with a chuckle. "Bobby, you've got the makings of a good Ranger. A man to ride the river with. Just don't ever get so hardened you don't regret taking another man's life."

"I sure hope I never do," Bobby answered. "Not to change the topic, but where are we gonna be tomorrow night?"

"We should make the Diamond SM spread by late afternoon. Sandoval Martone, its owner, is the man who got a bunch of his fellow cattlemen to send a letter to Austin, askin' for help. With any luck, he'll be able to give us more information than the sheriff back in Marfa did."

"Hell, he couldn't hardly give us any less," Bobby said.

"You've got that right," Luke answered. "Sheriff Clayton wasn't exactly cooperative. He said just enough to try and keep us from wondering whose side he's on. But it didn't work, leastwise as far as I'm concerned."

"Same goes for me," Bobby said.

"So we both read him the same way. That's good." Luke took a last drag on his quirly, then threw the butt into the fire. He drained the last of his coffee, and poured the dregs onto the coals.

"Let's call it a night."

"That'll be the main Diamond SM house, down in that little valley," Luke said to Bobby late the next afternoon, when they topped the summit of a low hill, and paused their horses. He pointed to a rambling adobe structure, surrounded by a verandah on all four sides. The thick walls and narrow, high up windows, would keep out all but the most determined raiders. Large pots of colorful flowers brightened the otherwise harsh exterior. Ristras of bright red, drying chiles hung from the beams. "They'll probably have guards watchin' out. Let's hope they don't have orders to shoot first and ask questions later."

"I'd feel a whole lot more comfortable if I could be certain of that," Bobby answered, with a wry grin.

"Well, if it makes you feel any better, we're about to find out," Luke replied. "Let's go."

They heeled their horses into a slow walk.

When they neared the open arch gateway to the ranch house yard, two men on horseback, holding rifles across the pommels of their saddles, blocked their way.

"Howdy, boys. Nice day, isn't it?" the one on the right said. "Y'all have any particular reason for trespassin' on Diamond SM land? If not, just turn around and go back wherever you came from. Or you'll get your hides ventilated. Keep your damn dog quiet, too," he added, when Blaze began to growl.

"Boy howdy. That ain't exactly a friendly welcome," Luke said.

"It wasn't intended to be." The cowboy lifted his rifle and pointed it at Luke's chest. "Raise your hands, both of you."

Luke and Bobby complied. They raised their hands shoulder-high.

"Now speak your piece, or git!"

"Senor Martone is expecting us," Luke answered, not blinking an eye.

"You're a damn liar," the other cowboy said. "Senor Martone would've told us if he was expectin' company."

"He didn't know when we'd get here, or even if," Luke answered. "Just tell him we came from Austin, in response to his letter. He'll know what that means."

"What d'ya think, Joe? Should we just blast these two outta their saddles and be done with it?" the first cowboy asked.

"I'm of a mind to, Hank. Sure don't want to bother Senor Martone with the likes of these two."

"If you do, I'll guarantee you Senor Martone won't be real happy about it," Luke answered. "In fact, I'm pretty certain you'd both be lookin' for new jobs."

"What'll we do, Joe?" Hank asked. "Mebbe these hombres are on the level."

"You *could* ask your boss," Luke suggested, with a half-grin on his face.

"I guess that'd be the thing to do, all right," Joe

said. To Luke and Bobby he continued. "You two just set. Don't even twitch, or we'll blow you to Kingdom Come."

Joe fired his rifle in the air, three times. Immediately, the heavy, carved oak front door swung open. Another cowboy holding a rifle stood in the entrance.

"What's goin' on, Joe?" he called.

"Got two strangers here claimin' they came to meet with Senor Martone. They say they're from Austin, and that the boss is expectin' 'em."

"Hold on a minute. I'll get him."

The door closed. Luke was certain that other armed men were at the windows, ready to shoot him and Bobby down at the first inkling they meant trouble. When the door reopened, Luke had to hide the surprise he felt. Along with the man who had answered the gunshots was another, a man not much older than himself. He wasn't dressed in the traditional clothing of a Mexican vaquero, much less a Spanish patron of a large rancho. Instead, he wore the outfit of a typical American rancher. He also held a newer model Winchester at the ready.

"Afternoon, gents," he said. "I'm Don Diego Sandoval de Vega Martone. I own every mile of land that you see around you. My segundo informs me you state that you have arrived from Austin, at my request. Is that correct?"

"It is, Senor Martone," Luke answered. "If

you'll permit me, I have papers which will prove that."

"Hank, let the man hand you his papers. Bring them to me," Martone ordered.

"They're in my saddlebags," Luke said. "I'll have to lower my hands to get them."

"Go ahead," Martone said. "I'm certain you realize if you make a stupid move my men will shoot you dead before you even have time to fall out of your saddle. Your compadre, also."

"I've no doubt of that," Luke answered.

"Get the papers, and give them to Hank."

"I just have to be certain no one will read them but you, Senor, before I do that."

"You have my word."

"Gracias."

Luke turned in his saddle, unstrapped the cover of his left saddlebag, and removed a thin, oilskin wrapped packet. He passed that to Hank, who rode up to the house, and handed it to his employer. Martone unwrapped the packet, and read through its contents.

"These are legitimate?" he asked Luke.

"They are. You should recognize the signature on the documents. I can confirm my identity, and my partner's, if you believe that's necessary."

"Not at all. Listen, all of you. These men are my guests. They will be treated as such. Gentlemen, please, come in. Tomas, see to the comfort of their animals. Make certain they are groomed,

158

fed, and watered. Fix their dog a place in the stable, with their horses," he ordered another man, who had emerged from the barn.

"Si, Don Sandoval," one of the vaqueros said. Once Luke and Bobby rode up to the door and dismounted, he took their horses' reins to lead them away. Blaze looked at Luke and whimpered.

"It's all right, Blaze," Luke reassured his dog. "Go with Pete and RePete."

"Gentlemen, mi casa su casa," Martone said. "But please, forgive my lack of manners. I have neglected to ask your names. Such a breach of etiquette is inexcusable."

"Mine is Luke Caldwell. My compadre's is Bobby Howell," Luke answered. "They're on our commissions, if you want to see them."

"I'm right pleased to make your acquaintance, Senor Martone," Bobby said.

"Nonsense. The pleasure is mine," Martone answered. "Also, everyone calls me Sandy, rather than Senor Martone, or Don Sandoval. Even the men you just met, when they are not dealing with strangers. The few who don't are vaqueros whose families have worked for the Diamond SM for as long as it has been in existence, which goes back many, many years before Texas was its own nation. They much prefer the old customs. I, on the other hand, look forward to progress, and all its possibilities. Follow me, por favor. You will rest and take refreshments, before we discuss business. That will come later, after dinner."

Martone led them down a long corridor, which was lined with gilt framed oil portraits of his ancestors. At the far end, he opened a door, which led to the hacienda's inner courtyard. Potted bougainvillea plants climbed the archway supports and covered sections of the walls and tile roof with their colorful bright red, pink, and magenta blooms. Hummingbirds flitted in and out of the plants, feeding on their sweet nectar. Other birds chirped in the manicured shrubs planted in the center of the courtyard, or splashed in the three tiered, central fountain. Wicker tables, chairs, and benches were strategically placed to catch the sun's warming rays, or the cooling shade, depending on the time of day and the weather.

"Luke, Bobby, you don't mind if I use your first names, do you?" Martone asked.

"Not at all, in fact I'd prefer that," Luke said.

Bobby nodded agreement.

"Good. Please, take seats at this table. I will send for something to quench your thirst, and fill your bellies. I'm certain you must be hungry and thirsty after your long ride."

"I could use a drink," Bobby admitted.

"You'll have one shortly."

Martone rang a bell that hung from the wall. A moment later, a dark-eyed, dark-haired young woman, clearly of Spanish heritage, dressed in a sleeveless white peasant blouse and a flowing, multi-colored striped skirt, appeared.

"You require something, Don Sandoval?" she asked.

"Si, Juanita. Vino y cigarros para mis invitados, por favor, y los pequenos pasteles tu madre hio esta manana."

"Si Don Sandoval. I will be but unos momentos."

"Gracias, Juanita."

The young woman made a slight curtsey, then went back inside.

"Juanita's family has been working for mine since my forebears first settled in the New World, shortly after the Conquistadores first explored this region," Martone explained. "Josephina, her madre, is our cook and housekeeper. Her padre, Juan, is my head wrangler. Her three brothers are all vaqueros. Just beyond the main stable and the men's bunkhouse, there is a compound of homes for the families who live and work on the ranch. We even have a chapel. A Padre comes over from Fort Davis once a month to say Mass."

"Sounds as if you should be able to handle any trouble thrown at you without needin' outside help, Sandy," Luke commented.

"Si, that is true," Martone admitted. "However, there are times a person can't handle a situation larger than himself, even with the help of Dios. Then, he must swallow his pride, or pay a high price for his arrogance. However, we won't talk of that now. Business can wait until after dinner. You're here, which means Austin hasn't ignored our plea, as myself and my fellow ranchers had feared. We had pretty much given up hope of hearing from the Rangers. For now, after we partake of Josephina's delicious cakes, fine wine and cigars, Juanita will show you to your rooms, and also where you may wash and change before our evening meal. You may take a siesta until then. One of the servants will summon you to the mesa. Ah, here's Juanita now."

The young servant woman was carrying a heavy tray of hammered silver, on which sat a newly opened bottle of wine, three cut-crystal glasses, three bone china plates, a jar holding cigars, and a platter of petite, delicately iced cakes. She put the tray down in the center of the table, smiling at Bobby.

"Will there be anything else, Don Sandoval?" she asked Martone.

"No, Juanita, that will be all. Please prepare two rooms for our guests. Return in una hora, por favor. They will be ready to wash and rest before supper by then. Gracias."

"Si, Don Sandoval."

Juanita curtsied again, smiled once more at Bobby, and left.

"I hope you'll enjoy this wine," Martone said. "It's a rare vintage Amontillado, which

I imported from Spain. I only open a bottle on special occasions."

He picked up the bottle and poured each glass half full.

"Take your glass, hold it in the palm of your hand, and swirl it so the wine can breathe, and bring out its true essence," Martone advised. "Also, you sip for the most enjoyment."

Luke and Bobby did as he advised, then each took tentative tastes.

"This is really good," Bobby said. "I've never had red-eye quite like this."

"Well, it's not exactly red-eye. Rot-gut neither," Martone answered, with a laugh. "Not at over one hundred dollars per bottle. But I understand your sentiments."

Luke nearly choked on the second sip he was taking.

"Over a hundred bucks a bottle?"

"Somewhat," Martone answered. "I have some vintages that are even more rare, and far costlier."

"Seems to me you must have enough money you could have hired your own private army to take on the renegades troublin' you," Luke said.

"Indeed I could have, but I prefer to do things within the law. That's why I advised my fellow ranchers to ask for Ranger help," he said. "No more talk of problems. Sample some of Juanita's splendid cakes. Then we'll have cigars. They're imported from Havana, Cuba. You won't find finer cigars anywhere in the world."

Luke and Bobby spent the next hour enjoying Martone's company. The descendant of Spanish nobility had no airs about him. He made his guests feel completely comfortable, as if they'd been acquainted for years. The minutes flew past. Before they realized an hour had gone by, Juanita had returned, to show them to their rooms.

Juanita took the Rangers down a long hallway, off either side of which were the guest bedrooms. She stopped in front of two open doors, opposite each other. She indicated the room on the left.

"Senor Caldwell, this is your room. Senor Howell, yours is the other. You will find robes and sandals laid out for you, along with wash-cloths, towels, and soap. There are also razors so you may shave, if you'd like. You will disrobe, por favor, and leave your soiled clothes on the floor at the foot of the bed. You will then put on the robes and sandals. I will wait here for you. When you have finished changing, I will show you where to bathe. Your soiled clothes will be removed to be laundered. New ones will be left in their place."

"Wait uno momento, senorita, por favor," Luke said. "Our spare outfits are in our saddlebags. Who would get them?"

"I said you will find new clothes awaiting you,"

Juanita answered. "Senor y Senora Sandoval keep a large supply of clothing on hand, for guests who may need any. These items will be gifts from la familia to you. They insist guests be properly attired at all times. You will also find your boots have been cleaned and polished while you bathe. Your sombreros will also be brushed."

"But . . . but I can't come out wearin' just a robe and huaraches in front of a girl, senorita," Bobby protested. "It wouldn't be decent."

"I assure you, nothing improper will happen," Juanita said.

"But, but you'll see my bare feet. The calves of my legs. Mebbe even a glimpse of my chest."

Juanita smiled disarmingly. It was plain she would enjoy catching a look at Bobby's chest or legs . . . or perhaps much more.

"Perhaps, Senor Howell. Is your chest so ugly a woman should not see it?"

"Yes. I mean, no. Aw, he . . . heck, I don't know what I mean," Bobby spluttered. "Luke, stop laughin'."

Luke was silently shaking with mirth at his new partner's discomfiture.

"You are wasting time, Senor. Surely you would like to take a siesta before dinner," Juanita insisted.

"I dunno about Bobby, but I sure would," Luke said.

"Excellent. It shouldn't take you long to change, once you get busy," Juanita said.

Bobby gave up the fight. He and Luke went into their rooms and shut the doors. As Juanita had promised, everything they needed was laid out for them. A few minutes later, they were back in the hallway. Luke couldn't help but notice Juanita sneaking a sly glance at Bobby's legs, then the tuft of thin, blond chest hair peeping out the top of his robe.

"This way, Senors," Juanita said. She led them out a back door, then around a rock wall to a hidden grotto. Water emerged from the base of a low wall, flowed several yards, then settled in a deep pool. From there, it flowed to another, lower pool, from whence it flowed away from the grotto, plunging over a cliff. Steam rose in clouds from the first pool, and less thickly from the second.

"Dios has blessed la familia Martone in many ways, including this hot spring," Juanita explained. "This is where the family and hacienda staff bathes. The waters are filled with rejuvenating minerals."

"Rejuvenating?" Bobby echoed.

"Si. Much like a tonic. They will soothe your aches and pains away, help you relax, and even pull poisons from your body."

"Juanita seems to know more English words that you do there, pardner," Luke teased.

"Senora Sandoval insists everyone on the hacienda staff is fluent in both Inglesa y Espanol," Juanita explained. "Now, I will leave you to your baths. The door will be left unlocked, so when you are finished, you may return to your rooms for siestas. A servant will summon you for dinner, which is at eight o'clock."

"But, what if someone comes by?" Bobby questioned.

"No one will," Juanita assured him. "However, if someone mistakenly did, I am certain the view would be quite pleasant, if that someone was a woman, that is."

Bobby flushed deep red.

"Pard, you're red as a beet, and you ain't even been in that hot water yet," Luke said.

Bobby glared daggers at him.

Even after hearing the door close behind Juanita, Bobby looked around several times before he slipped out of his robe. Luke had already settled neck deep into the steaming first pool.

"About time you got in here, Bobby," he said. "This is heaven on Earth."

"It does feel mighty fine on my achin' muscles," Bobby agreed. "Still can't believe I let that gal see me half naked."

"You weren't anywhere near half naked," Luke pointed out. "Besides, I caught you takin' a gander at her chest, too."

Bobby blushed again. The stirring in his groin and the blood racing through his veins made it clear it wasn't just the hot water turning his face crimson.

"Yeah. Wouldn't that really be somethin', if you could just disappear for a while, Luke, and Juanita was next to me here in this spring instead?"

"You tryin' to say I'm not good-lookin'?" Luke challenged.

"I didn't pay no never mind, one way or the other," Bobby retorted. "But you damn sure don't have curves like Juanita's got, and you sure as hell don't have the right parts."

"I'll give you that," Luke said. "Boy howdy, it's gonna feel good losing five pounds of dirt off my hide, and getting all slicked up for dinner."

"This place sure is fancy, all right," Bobby said. "I can't quite put my finger on how these folks talk, though. Their English, especially Sandy's, seems awful high-falutin' and stuffy most times, but then they'll start talkin' regular, like us."

"Quite a few folks in this part of Texas speak like that," Luke explained. "Especially the old Spanish families. They're used to talking much more formally, mostly in Spanish. So their speech comes out as a jumble of Mexican, Texan, and maybe even a bit of Indian tossed in for good measure. I am gonna give you one piece of advice, though."

"What's that, Luke?"

"No matter what that little gal Juanita does, of if you happen to find yourself alone with her, don't even think of touching her. You do, and you'll spend the rest of your life as a gelding . . . if you're lucky."

Bobby swallowed hard.

"You made that pretty plain."

"Just wanted to make certain you know where things stand around here. I'm gonna start scrubbin'."

Luke reached for the bar of soap at the edge of the pool.

Luke and Bobby were awakened by sharp raps on their doors. They hurriedly dressed in the new clothes they'd been provided. Waiting for them was a middle-aged, plump Mexican woman, wearing a severe, high collared, floor length wide skirted black dress.

"I am Maria. You will follow me to the dining room, por favor."

As they walked down the hall, she glared at Bobby.

"I am Juanita's tia, her duena. I have seen the way you look at her, with lust in your eyes. I warn you, if you so much as harm a hair on her head, I will slice you into little pieces and feed you to the cerdos." Without waiting for Bobby to answer, she looked straight ahead.

She led them into a large, high ceilinged room, decorated with Spanish and Mexican antiques. In the center of the room was a large, elaborately carved walnut dining table and chairs. It was set with heavy silverware and delicate, floral patterned bone china plates and serving pieces. The Martones had already gathered. They stood up when the Rangers entered the room.

"Ah, you are right on time," Martone said. "Permit me to introduce mi familia. This is mi esposa, Estrella Lucia." Senora Martone was a striking, raven haired beauty. "Mi ninos are Esteban, Emilio, Paolo, and Juan. Mi ninas are Consuela, Rosa, and Domenica."

The children ranged in age from about thirteen down to two.

After the greetings were exchanged and everyone acknowledged, Martone ordered everyone to sit down.

"First, we will say la Gracia. Rosa, it is your turn to lead us."

Everyone bowed their heads. The Martones made the Sign of the Cross when Rosa began praying, "En el nombre de Padre, y del Hijo, y del Espiritu Santo. Amen. Benedicenos, O Senor, y benedico estes tus dones, que estamos a punto de recibir de tu generosidad, por Christo nuestro Senor. Amen."

Once the prayer was concluded, Martone picked up a silver bell and tinkled it. A steady stream of servants entered and exited the kitchen, beginning the meal with bowls of gazpacho soup.

The main course was roast beef, accompanied, in the Mexican culinary tradition, with tortillas and rice rather than potatoes and bread. The meal went on for over two hours, running the gamut of items from A to Z; aquacates, avocadoes, to zanahorias, carrots. It was almost ten-thirty when the final course, Mexican flan for dessert, was served.

"I hope both you senors found the food satisfactory, and sufficient," Senora Martone said.

"It was delicious," Luke answered. "I can't possibly eat another crumb."

"I don't believe I've ever had such a wonderful meal," Bobby answered. "Muchas gracias."

"I'm so glad you were pleased," Senora Martone answered.

"Now, gentlemen, we will take our leave, and retire to the library for cigars and brandy," Martone said.

Luke and Bobby made their good nights, then followed their host to the walnut paneled library. Martone shut the door behind them.

"As soon as we have our glasses filled and our cigars lit, we can get to the business at hand."

Luke and Bobby took seats on a hunter green leather sofa. Martone sat in a chair of the same color and material opposite them. They all held snifters of brandy and long, thick cigars.

"I know you must have plenty of questions," Martone said. "I'll answer them best as I can."

"Sure, Sandy. You've compiled a pretty extensive list of the predations being done in this territory," Luke said. "It appears the local law has been completely baffled in their search for those responsible."

"They have," Martone answered. "They've been runnin' themselves ragged, chasin' their own tails goin' around in circles, while the outlaws are laughing their fool heads off at 'em. Of course, it would help if the sheriff actually had his posses look in the right direction."

"What do you mean? He told us pretty specifically that the main gang has a hideout somewhere southeast of here, about thirty miles or so."

"Sheriff Wilbur Clayton is a stubborn, stupid cabron. The main group, or groups, hole up northwest of here, in the Davis Mountains. He's been told that many times."

"Then why would he tell us different?"

"Quien sabe, Luke? Perhaps there is another renegade outfit down southeast of here. But the men running roughshod over the people here come out of the Davis Mountains. They hit fast, then disappear back into the mountain range. You are no doubt aware that is extremely rugged terrain. There must be literally hundreds of places where men on the run from the law can hide."

"Has anyone ever gone in there after 'em, Sandy?" Bobby asked.

"Si. Whoever has tried was never seen again. My former neighbor, Josh Jackson, pursued the outlaws with his entire crew, after his ranch was attacked. Twenty-two men went into the mountains, not one has ever returned."

"One thing doesn't make sense," Luke said. "Fort Davis is right outside those mountains. Has the Army gotten involved?"

"Only as far as they are allowed. The Army is still here to protect travelers and freighters on the Trans-Pecos segment of the San Antonio-El Paso Road, and the Chihuahua Trail. They're also supposed to keep the Indians in check on the Great Comanche War Trail, and the Mescalero Apache War Trails. As you know, the Army isn't allowed to get involved with enforcing the law on Whites, or even Mexicans or Negroes. They've also lost a few men searching for raiders, and haven't been completely successful is stopping raids on stagecoaches and emigrant wagons. You won't be able to count on them for assistance."

"That don't matter," Luke said. "The Rangers and the United States Army still don't get along all that well. Bobby, it seems like me'n you are gonna be headed into the Davises, startin' tomorrow morning."

"May I say something, Luke?" Martone asked.
"Go ahead."

"We had requested an entire troop of Rangers. How are just the two of you going to be able to fight a force that outnumbers you by perhaps ten or fifteen to one, even more?"

"That's where we'll have the advantage," Luke answered. "A troop would be too easy to spot. The men we're after could observe every movement, then either just fade away into the malpais, or lay an ambush. With just two of us, we should be able to work our way right up to their camp. We can pick off a few on our way, if we get the chance. Then, we'll let surprise do the rest. The only thing I'm worried about is why the sheriff tried to steer us in the wrong direction. If he's in cahoots with the gangs, and has already managed to get word to them about us, our job will be that much harder. Unless you've got any more questions or information, Sandy, me'n Bobby are gonna call it a night. We'll get an early start come morning."

"Of course. All I have to say is buena suerte, y que Dios te proteja."

12

The Davis Mountains were a half day's ride from the Diamond SM. Since riding too deep into those rugged ridges, ravines and canyons after dark would be sheer suicide, Luke intended to get as far into the mountains as he could before dusk, then find a good secluded spot to make camp.

"Bobby," he said, as they wound their way deeper into the mountains, "you might be about to face a bunch of desperate, vicious men, mebbe even some Apaches, but no matter how many we've got to fight, you'll still be safer than you were at the Martone spread."

"Just what do you mean by that, Luke?"

"Juanita. Sooner or later that gal would have gotten you into her bed. If she had, you'd have been a dead man. The Spanish have a strong sense of honor. It wouldn't matter to her family, or the Martones, whether or not she was willing. You'd never have left that rancho alive. Her ma and pa probably have already arranged a marriage for her."

"Why? That doesn't happen nowadays."

"Old traditions die hard in some societies. The people descended from the Spanish nobility still hold to those customs."

Bobby took off his hat to wipe sweat from his brow. He stiffened in the saddle.

"Somethin' wrong?" Luke asked.

"Mebbe, but I sure hope not. I think I just saw an Indian, up on the rimrock where that slot cuts into it."

"Are you certain?"

"Not one hundred percent, but I wouldn't wager against it."

"Don't act like you suspect anything. Just keep riding. We'll keep our eyes peeled."

"As long as any Indians don't capture us, and peel back our eyelids for us," Bobby answered, with a bitter laugh.

They rode for another half mile. This time it was Luke who spotted an Indian, lying flat on the edge of a high cliff.

"You were right, Bobby. There's another one, up among the rocks. Must be a Mescalero. And where there's one, there'll be more."

"Kinda funny they're lettin' us see 'em."

"If they're lettin' us see them, they want us to seem 'em," Luke replied. "If they didn't, we'd have no clue they were following us."

"But why?"

"To make us sweat. Mescaleros are real good at gettin' inside an enemy's head. They'll have an ambush set up somewhere ahead. If we try to turn back and run for it, they'll have men waitin' to cut us off. If we keep on goin', they know we'll have to ride straight into their trap. The longer they keep us guessin', the more likely it is we'll get nervous. And nervous men make mistakes. We've got to stay calm if we have any chance at all of makin' it through their trap alive."

"Tell that to my guts," Bobby said. "They're already churnin'."

"And I've got a lump of ice sittin' in my belly," Luke answered. "That doesn't matter. What we have to do is keep our heads clear."

"And our scalps attached to 'em."

"They'll go after yours first. Taking a blond scalp is considered powerful medicine."

"Oh, *that's* a real comfort."

"I thought it would be," Luke said. Blaze had wandered ahead, following a scent. Luke whistled him back.

"You've gotta stick close with us for a spell, pal," he told the dog. Blaze gave a soft bark in reply.

Half a mile on, there were four Mescaleros in plain sight, two each riding horseback on the rimrock on both sides of the pass. They were matching their pace to that of the Rangers. Occasionally, one would shake his lance or bow, and let loose a war cry.

"They're funneling us into an ambush all right, Bobby," Luke said. "If we want to get out of it with our hides not ventilated, and our scalps still attached, we've got to figure out how to spring their trap before it's set."

"Assuming we can figure out where they're waitin' for us," Bobby answered.

"That's right. I've fought Indians before. I can usually pick out where they plan to fight. They're not worried about us gettin' away. They figure they've got us cornered, and probably panicked. We might be able to use that to our advantage."

They rode another quarter mile, to where the pass narrowed and curved, pinching the trail between two talus slopes of tumbled boulders and downed trees. The Mescaleros on the rimrocks had vanished.

"There. That's where those sons of bitches are gonna hit us, Bobby," Luke said. "It's an ideal spot. Keep moving, until just before we reach the narrows. Then, dig your spurs into your horse's flanks, duck low, and ride like hell. With luck, we'll be past those Indians before they start shootin'. We won't be able to outrun 'em. Soon as we get into the rocks, get off your horse and take cover. We'll have a chance to hold 'em off if we do. Even better, they might stop and try'n grab our horses, before they come after us. Those Apaches'll be mighty curious about what's in my packsaddle. Probably hoping they'll find some firewater. We can pick some of 'em off if they do."

"Sounds like we need a miracle," Bobby said.

"I'm already prayin' for one. Let's go."

They kept their horses at a steady trot until they

reached the landslides. With a yell, they jammed their spurs deep into their horses' sides, sending them into a deep run. Blaze stayed alongside Luke, tongue lolling as he raced with his owner.

The Mescaleros had indeed been surprised by the Rangers' unexpected move. They sent a few bullets and arrows at their elusive targets as Luke and Bobby raced into the defile, urging their horses on.

When they got into the thick of the narrows, Luke and Bobby grabbed their rifles and rolled from their saddles. Their horses kept running through the gap in the walls. The Rangers scrambled into rock nests, Bobby on the left of the trail, Luke on the right.

The Mescaleros who had been hazing them from the cliffs had gone past and circled back. They charged into the gap, where they made easy targets for Luke and Bobby, who, behind their protective boulders, shot the Indians out of their saddles. There were others, though, hidden among the same rocks where the Rangers had taken cover. Luke had no idea of their numbers.

"Make certain of every shot!" he shouted to Bobby. Bobby waved his rifle in answer.

The Indians were working their way closer to Luke and Bobby's positions. Arrows and bullets began seeking the Rangers out. One Apache made the mistake of exposing his shoulder. Luke put a bullet through it, shattering the joint. When the Apache fell from behind a downed tree, Luke drilled him through the top of his skull. His shot enraged the Apaches, who charged, indifferent to the bullets coming at them. Several went down, but five made it to the Rangers' positions, and overran them. Bobby reversed his empty rifle and clubbed one of the two attacking him across the gut, breaking several ribs. The Apache went down, twisting onto his back. Bobby grabbed the man's knife and jammed it deep into his belly. The Indian screamed. Before Bobby could make certain he was dead, the second Apache was on him. Bobby shifted just in time to avoid a fatal blow to the back of his skull from the Indian's war club. He took the blow on his right shoulder, leaving it paralyzed with pain. He dropped the knife he held, scrambling in a desperate attempt to avoid a second, fatal crushing blow to his head.

On the other side of the trail, Luke had tossed aside his rifle and drawn his Peacemaker. He got off one shot, which took the nearest Apache just above his belly button. The Indian collapsed atop Luke, who shoved him aside. The two remaining Mescaleros grabbed Luke, one by each arm. They started to drag him over the rocks.

Blaze had disappeared, but Luke was too occupied fighting the Indians to worry about his dog. Now, the pup appeared on top of a boulder, growling, his teeth bared. He jumped, clamping his teeth down on one Indian's arm. He locked his jaw, dragging the man off Luke. The other Mescalero, panicked at the sudden vision of what he believed to be a wolf, loosened his grasp on Luke's arm. Luke kicked him in the right knee, shattering the kneecap. The Indian fell, his left temple slamming against the sharp corner of a jagged rock. Bone crunched. Blood spurted from the Indian's temple, poured from his mouth, nose, and ears. He collapsed on his belly and lay still.

Blaze had let go of his grip on the other Mescalero's arm. He now had the Apache by the throat, his jaw locked. Blood flowing from severed blood vessels soaked the dog's muzzle. He held on, shaking the Indian violently. When the renegade finally stopped his struggles, Blaze turned him loose. The Indian's throat was ripped wide open.

"Good work, Blaze," Luke told the dog. "You saved my bacon. I'll buy you the biggest steak I can find next town we get to. We'd better check on Bobby. Let's hope there's no more of these bastards hidin' in the rocks."

Staying low, Luke shouted for his partner. He received a weak call in reply.

"Where you at?" Luke shouted.

"Behind that big red boulder. I'm all right, but can use a little help."

"Be right there."

Luke got up and crossed the trail. When he

circled the boulder, he found Bobby with his foot wedged in a crack in the rocks. The body of his second attacker, his skull split in two like a ripe melon, lay atop the young Ranger.

"I'm here," Luke said.

"Get this son of a bitch off me," Bobby said. "My foot's caught under a rock, too. I need help workin' it out."

"I'll get you free quick as I can."

Luke pushed the dead Mescalero's body aside, then carefully maneuvered Bobby's foot until it came free.

"Think you can stand up?" Luke asked. "Feel like there's any broken bones?"

"Nah, I'm just a bit banged up. Blood on me's from the Indian I gutted. Damn, he ruined my nice new shirt the Martones gave me. How about you? And Blaze? Looks like he tangled with a bear."

"I'm fine. Just a little beat up, like you. But if Blaze hadn't finished off one of these hombres, I'd be bald right now. We'd better get movin'. Sooner or later, these braves'll be missed. We don't want to be anywhere near this place when their friends find 'em."

Bobby stood up. He retrieved his rifle. He and Luke walked back to the road. Luke gave a sharp whistle. Pete and RePete came out of the brush, along with Tony. None of the horses seemed the worse for wear.

"We'll check the bodies, to make certain they're all dead," Luke said. "Then we'll strip the gear from their ponies and turn the animals loose. They'll either be picked up by another band of Mescaleros, or go back to the wild."

They examined the bodies littering the gap. None of the Indians had survived. Their deadly ambush had turned into a death trap for them.

"You reckon one of these is Victorio?" Bobby asked.

Luke shook his head.

"Nope. If this had been Victorio's band, me'n you wouldn't be standing here talkin' right now. We'd be the ones lyin' dead. The only difference is our scalps would've been lifted, our bellies sliced open, guts pulled out and our innards stuffed with grass and rocks. Worst, our man parts cut off and shoved in our mouths."

"You mean like prairie oysters?" Bobby said.

"That's exactly what I mean. And we would have still been alive when they cut 'em off."

Bobby gagged.

"We got real lucky. These were all young bucks. Looks like they decided to try'n make their first kills, or try'n count their first coups. If these had been seasoned warriors, we wouldn't have had a prayer. Let's get goin', before we're found here. Blaze, you're gonna ride on RePete for the rest of the day. You've worked hard enough."

"Hang on a second, Luke," Bobby said.

The young Ranger went to one of the dead Mescaleros. He took the bow still clasped in the Indian's hand, and his quiver of arrows. He slung those over his own shoulder.

"What're you takin' those for, Bobby?" Luke asked. "It ain't right takin' trophies from the dead."

"I'm not disagreein' with you, Luke," Bobby answered. "But these might come in handy."

"You really believe that?"

"Quien sabe? But better to have 'em and not need 'em than need 'em and not have 'em."

"I suppose," Luke said. "Let's scatter these ponies and get outta here. The buzzards'll start circlin' anytime now. We don't want another band of Mescaleros to get curious about what those scavengers saw and catch us still here."

Once the Indians' ponies were turned loose, the Rangers resumed their journey. They needed to put as many miles as possible between them and the site of the ambush before dark.

13

The two Rangers criss-crossed through the Davis Mountains for three days before they found the first sign of the men they were searching for. The tracks of a large number of shod horses led from three burnt out freight wagons, into a long canyon. The only remains of the freighters, and their mules, were their scavenger picked bones.

"Those look like they probably belong to the men Sandy told us about, Bobby," Luke said. "Seems like it's just about time to start really earning our pay."

"Which I haven't got yet," Bobby reminded him, with a chuckle.

"If our luck runs out, you won't have to worry about your money," Luke answered.

"We goin' after 'em right now?"

Luke looked up at the westering sun.

"I doubt we'll catch up with those sons of bitches before sundown. I'd rather not get into a gun battle where we'll be outnumbered in the dark. Too many chances for them to slip by us, and get away. Or one of us to shoot the other by mistake."

"If that canyon's not a box we won't catch up with the outfit until tomorrow anyway," Bobby pointed out.

"True. But I have a feeling it isn't. Those hombres wouldn't want to travel at night either, unless they realized someone is on their trail. There's also lots of faint, older tracks on this trail, both comin' and goin'. I'd wager their hideout is at the end of this canyon. Easy to guard, and easy to defend."

"Tracks which they sure aren't tryin' to hide."

"That's another reason not to trail 'em at night. They most likely know every inch of these mountains. We don't. They could be camped for the night, and we could ride right on by 'em, without knowin' it, until it was too late. Or we could stumble smack into the bunch. They ain't tryin' to hide their tracks because they've been robbin' and killin' for so long now, they figure they can get away with it as long as they want. That's about to change."

"Luke, this is just a guess, but judging from the hoof prints, I'd say we'll be goin' up against twenty men, more or less. Those are mighty long odds."

"Not for the Rangers. Ten to one is just about right. You are right about one thing. We can't just go in there shootin' and expect to come out alive. You can also be certain if we ask those bastards to pretty please hand over their guns and surrender, they'd laugh their fool heads off. We have to outsmart 'em."

"Mebbe that would work. They'd die laughin',"

Bobby answered. "Seriously, Luke, do you have any kind of a plan?"

"I will once we can size up the situation. For now, we'll follow the trail as far as we dare, then stop for the night. We'll have a cold camp. Soon as it's light enough, we'll start out again. If we're real lucky, they might not have gone much farther ahead of us. If we could hit them not too much after sunup, we might catch most of 'em still sleeping, especially if those wagons were haulin' whiskey. The attack happened no more than a couple of days ago. The scavengers picked the victims' bones clean, but they ain't scattered 'em yet. If the hombres we're after are like most renegades, they'll have gone on a good drinkin' tear once they reached their hideout. That'll be to our advantage. Let's get movin'. The sun's sinking fast, and I want to make certain we find some good cover for the night."

The sun had just topped the eastern horizon, gilding the thin clouds in pastels of pink, yellow, and orange, when Luke and Bobby broke camp. The morning mist still hung in the air. Birds flitted in the trees, chirping their greetings to the new day. Squirrels scampered from branch to branch, chattering. It would have been a beautiful morning, if the Rangers had not been riding against a gang of vicious killers. Before this day was out, neither might still be alive.

They rode silently, the only sounds besides the wild creatures the clopping of their horses' hooves, the creak of saddle leather, and the jingling of bit chains. They'd been in the saddle for about an hour when Luke reined up.

"Hold on, Bobby. There's somethin' up ahead. I want to get a closer look."

Luke rummaged in his saddlebags and took out his field glasses. He put them to his eyes, focused, then grunted.

"What've you got, Luke?" Bobby asked.

"Two men on guard, one on each side of the canyon, about a quarter mile ahead. I don't think they've seen us, yet. Their view of the trail is still partly screened by the trees and brush. But once we're past that last grove of redberry junipers, we might as well have targets painted on our shirts."

"You mind if I take a look?"

"No, but let's get off this trail and into the brush first."

They pushed their horses into the thorny vegetation. Luke handed Bobby the glasses.

"Let's see," Bobby said, as he peered into the distance. "Two men, both on rocks, about twenty feet above the trail. One on each side, like you said. And hardly any cover between us and them."

"We've got to figure a way to take them out, before they can give a warning," Luke said. "We can't just shoot 'em, because the gunshots would give us away. If there was a way to sneak up on 'em, we'd have to strangle them, or slit their throats, so they couldn't scream."

"We could come up behind them, cover their mouths, and stab 'em in the back," Bobby suggested.

Luke shook his head.

"Too risky. If we don't catch them by complete surprise, they'll put up a fight. It could be us takin' a knife in the guts, instead of them."

Bobby looked at the guards, and the terrain, through the glasses again.

"I've got an idea, Lieutenant."

"Lieutenant? Not Luke? That must be one helluva idea."

"It's a long shot, but probably the only one we've got. Remember I said the bow and arrows I took off that dead Mescalero might come in handy?"

"Yeah. What're you gettin' at?"

"I'm certain I can belly my way through the brush, and get close enough to down both those hombres with arrows."

"Without them screamin' when they get hit?"

"Where I plan to hit them, they won't be able to scream. There's only one hitch in the plan."

"Only one?" Luke was dubious.

"Well, only one *major* hitch. That's where you come in, Lieutenant. I need you to act as bait. You'll have to ride straight up the trail like

189

you ain't got a care in the world, to draw those hombres out to where I can have a clear shot at them."

"Are you serious?"

"Dead serious. Unless you can come up with another idea."

"Lemme think on this a minute."

Luke mulled the situation over in his mind. He could see no possible way of getting past the guards, or killing them, without alarming the rest of the gang. The only alternative, one a Texas Ranger would never consider, would be to turn back, and get more help. By the time they returned, the outlaws would probably be long gone. Bobby was right. They had no choice.

"Are you positive you can get both of those hombres, before they start shootin' at me?" Luke asked.

"You want to place a small wager?"

"I'm already bettin' my life."

"I reckon you are, at that. Yes, I'm positive. I'm also certain neither one of them will make more than a grunt when they drop."

"How much time do you need?"

"Give me fifteen minutes to get in position. I should be able to see you coming a moment or two before the guards do."

"All right. I will have my rifle out, though, just in case something goes wrong. If I have to use it, well, things could get ugly."

"You won't," Bobby assured him. "Just bring Tony along for me. It'll save backtrackin' to pick him up once I'm done."

"All right."

"I'm goin' now. Wish me luck," Bobby said.

"I'm the one who's gonna need the luck," Luke retorted.

Bobby grinned, then plunged into the brush. Luke waited the requested fifteen minutes, while Bobby wriggled his way into the place he wanted.

"Here goes," Luke muttered. With Blaze trotting alongside him, he put Pete into a walk, with RePete and Tony trailing behind. He rode with his Winchester in his right hand, lying against his leg, ready to swing up and use in an instant. He murmured a silent prayer things wouldn't come to that.

When he came into the guards' field of vision, the man on the left spotted him first. He scrambled to his feet. Before he could get into action, an arrow pierced his neck from side to side, tearing through his larynx and windpipe. He dropped his rifle, grabbed his throat, fell to the rocks, and writhed in agony, as his life blood drained from his torn open throat. The second guard, seeing his partner go down, attempted to yell a warning. When he opened his mouth, an arrow went through it, slicing his tongue in two, then snapping his spine when it exited the back of his neck. He toppled back, sliding into a thicket of ocotillo and prickly pear. The only sign he had ever been present was a slight dust cloud, which soon dissipated.

"I'm comin' out, Luke, don't shoot me!" Bobby called.

Luke had stopped in the middle of the trail, staring dumbfounded at the first guard's body.

"You all right, Luke?" Bobby asked, grinning, and he emerged from the brush.

"I am now," Luke answered. "Damn. Where'd you learn to aim a bow and arrow like that?"

"Had some practice when I was a kid," Bobby answered. "Told you they wouldn't yell out, didn't I? And that the bow and arrows might come in handy?"

"You sure as hell did, but I never would've believed you could put an arrow into a man's throat from that far off. You sure you ain't part Indian?"

"Do I look like it?" Bobby asked.

"No, I reckon not," Luke conceded. "Unless you're the whitest damn redskin on God's green earth. Enough talk. We'd better get movin' and see what else we're gonna be facin'. Someone might come along to relieve those two hombres any time now. We'll ride as far as it seems prudent, then go the rest of the way on foot."

He handed Bobby his horse's reins. Bobby mounted, and they began moving forward.

Bobby started reciting Alfred, Lord Tennyson's *The Charge of the Light Brigade.*

"Half a league, half a league, half a league onward, all in the Valley of Death, rode the six hundred. 'Forward the Light Brigade! Charge for the guns!' he said. Into the Valley of Death, rode the six hundred . . ."

"What the hell is that you're mumbling?" Luke asked.

"*The Charge of the Light Brigade.* It's a poem, by a Britisher, Alfred, Lord Tennyson. And no, you don't want to know how it turns out."

A short distance after the guard's post, the canyon took a sharp bend to the right.

"Here's where we leave the horses, and continue on foot," Luke said. He dismounted, followed by Bobby. They led the horses into a crevice in the canyon's left wall, and let their reins drop. A spring emanated from the crevice, giving enough moisture so there was plenty of grass for the animals to crop, as well as a small waterhole. With enough grazing and water, the horses would stay put. Luke ordered Blaze to remain with the horses.

"Take off your spurs, and anythin' else that might make noise, Bobby," Luke ordered. "Stuff as many cartridges in your pockets as you can."

They removed their spurs, and hung them from their saddle horns. Luke took his badge from his pocket and pinned it to his vest. After filling their pockets with ammunition, and taking their rifles, Bobby also the bow and remaining arrows, they began a slow walk through the brush. After a few hundred feet, Luke put out his hand, holding Bobby back.

"Get down," he hissed. "The place is right in front of us."

He and Bobby dropped to their bellies, and wormed their way to where the canyon widened to a small valley. A large cabin was situated against the valley's headwall. To its right was a large barn, to its left a corral filled with horses. Behind the corral was an open-fronted hay shed.

"From the size of that cabin, Bobby, it seems you were right about how many men we'll be goin' up against. Damn, I was hopin' you were wrong," Luke whispered. "As least it looks like no one's awake yet. That's one thing in our favor."

"What about ten to one odds bein' just about right for the Rangers?" Bobby asked, also keeping his voice low to avoid any chance of it echoing off the surrounding cliffs.

"I lied," Luke said. He looked over the cabin and its surroundings. "We damn sure can't just go chargin' in on those hombres. We'd be shot to pieces before we got anywhere near the building." He studied the valley more closely for a few moments, then looked at Bobby.

"How many arrows have you got left in that quiver?"

"Five. Why? You got an idea?"

"Mebbe. Do you think you can put a couple of fire arrows into the cabin's front windows? Then one into the hay in the shed?"

Bobby estimated the distance. He licked his thumb and held it in the air.

"Yeah, I believe I can. It'll be quite a shot, but the wind's, what little of it there is, at our backs. That'll help."

"Bueno. I'm gonna work my way around to the corral. Give me ten minutes. Your job is to put those arrows where I said. Soon as the hay takes hold, I'll turn the horses loose and scatter 'em. If most of those hombres are still asleep, the fire should panic them. Between the smoke, flames, and noise from the horses, those sons of bitches will be really confused. We'll be ready to cut them down as they run out of the cabin."

"Just a minute. What're we gonna use for fuel?"

"Our neckerchiefs. Gimme yours, and three arrows."

"We've only got two neckerchiefs," Bobby pointed out.

"We'll tear 'em. I've got an extra with me. We'll tear that one into strips to tie the rags in place. I've got a flask of whiskey in my back pocket. Don't ask me why I grabbed it, because I sure don't know why. We'll wrap the rags to the arrows, tie them in place, and soak them. With any luck, at least one of them you put through the windows will land on something that catches fire, real quick."

"Not gonna give 'em a chance to surrender? I know, just asking," Bobby said, when Luke gave him a withering look.

"We're way outnumbered, the tracks from the outfit which attacked the freighters led us straight here, so those men inside are guilty as sin. No, we're not. No point puttin' this off. The longer we stall, the more likely it is those hombres'll start stirrin', and mebbe see us. If this don't work, I'll see you on the other side."

"It'll work," Bobby said. "Just have a feelin', deep in my gut, that it will."

"Better hope that feelin' doesn't turn into a bullet in your gut," Luke answered, with a grim chuckle. "Ten minutes."

Luke was almost in position when a man came out of the cabin. Luke froze, hoping against hope the man wouldn't spot him. He watched while the outlaw walked up to a tree, unbuttoned his pants, and began to relieve himself. Luke tried to hug the ground more closely, but his boot snapped a dry twig. The crack sounded loud as a gunshot in the morning quiet. The outlaw turned, and stared straight at Luke. Before he could react, Luke pulled his Bowie out of its sheath. He threw the knife. The heavy blade buried itself deep in the outlaw's belly. Luck was with Luke. The man didn't scream when the knife struck. He just grunted, looked dumbly at the knife protruding from his gut, staggered into the tree, and slumped to the dirt.

"Aw, hell!" Bobby hissed. "That blows Luke's plan sky high."

He notched one arrow to the bow, and pulled the string. The arrow flew straight and true, crashing through a lower pane of one window. He hastily notched and sent a second arrow flying. This one embedded itself in the other window's frame. The cabin's dry wood quickly took flame. Bobby's third arrow landed in the midst of the hay. The slight breeze gave more life to the flames. They eagerly licked at the hay.

Keeping low, Luke raced for the corral gate. He flung it open, then emptied his pistol into the air. The horses, already terrified by the blazing hay, galloped out of the corral. Luke dove to his belly behind a water trough.

Shots and curses were coming from the cabin. Something Bobby's first arrow landed on had burst into flames, which were now boiling out of the window. The cabin door burst open, as the men inside fled the thick, choking smoke and heat.

"No point in wastin' these," Bobby muttered. He put one arrow into an outlaw's chest. His last struck another man in the stomach. He stumbled for several steps, then pitched to his face. Bobby tossed aside the bow, grabbed his rifle, and added his shooting to that of Luke.

Only two or three of the outlaws managed to get off wild shots, before Ranger lead cut them down. Silence descended on the valley, broken only by the squawking of crows and the whinnies of nervous horses. Luke and Bobby cautiously came into the open. The cabin was now engulfed in flames. Anyone still inside had no chance of survival.

"You all right?" Luke called.

"Yeah. You?"

"Yep. We'd better check these hombres to make certain of 'em. Then, I'm real curious about what's in that other building."

They examined the bodies lying on the ground. Thirteen men lay dead.

"I reckon the others never made it out," Bobby said.

"I reckon," Luke agreed. "Let's see what's inside that barn."

Luke reloaded his Colt as they walked toward the barn. Without warning, the hayloft door swung open. Three men were bunched together in the loft. When they opened fire, two others, on horseback, galloped from behind the barn, shooting as they raced away. One bullet caught Bobby in his chest. As he was falling, Bobby put a bullet through the shooter's gut. The man doubled over and fell from the loft. Luke was clipped across the top of his shoulder. His return shots took out both remaining men. They plunged to the ground, alongside their dying companion.

Bobby was lying face down. Luke knelt alongside him, and rolled him onto his back.

"How bad you hit?" he asked.

"Feels pretty . . . bad," Bobby gasped. "How about you?"

"I caught one across my shoulder. Hurts like hell, and I'm bleedin' like a stuck pig, but I should be fine."

"My chest is . . . on fire," Bobby said. He moaned. "Least I . . . got the son of a bitch who . . . got me."

"Lemme take a look."

Luke opened Bobby's shirt. The wound was high on the right side of his chest. Luke listened, but didn't hear any sucking sound, which would indicate that the bullet had punctured a lung.

"Well?"

"It's bad, all right. But there is some good news. I don't think the slug hit any vitals. There's no blood frothin' from your mouth, or leaking from your nose or ears. The trouble is, the slug's still in you, and I'm certain it's too deep for me to dig out. I'm gonna plug the hole as best I can, then get the horses. You've got to get to a doc as fast as possible. You think you'll be able to ride?"

"I . . . can try."

"Bueno. If you can't, I'll tie you in your saddle. It's gonna be rough on you, but if we push hard, we can make Marfa by nightfall."

"What about the . . . ones that . . . got away?"

"We can't worry about them now. They're long gone. Mebbe we'll figure out who they are and catch up with 'em later."

"Luke?"

"Yeah?"

"Did you notice . . . anythin' about those three . . . hombres in the barn?"

"You mean that they were in Army shirts and hats? Two of them were Black? Buffalo soldiers? I damn for sure did."

"At least I got . . . the bastard who . . . plugged me. Wonder why . . . Army."

"Keep quiet. Save your strength."

"But."

"But we'll probably find out those hombres were crooked soldiers. That would explain why the gang never was caught, until now. They had inside information about where the patrols would be. Now, just lie still. I'll be right back with the horses."

"I sure as hell . . . ain't goin' . . . nowhere," Bobby said. He smiled, then passed out.

14

Luke rode into Marfa just after dark. Bobby had drifted in and out of consciousness for the entire trip, so Luke had tied him to his horse. He rode straight through town, to Doctor Lewis Bunting's office. The doctor took Bobby right in, assured Luke he would do everything he could for the young Ranger, then ordered him out of the office, with a promise he would get word to Luke as soon as he was finished operating. At that time, he would also treat Luke's wounded shoulder.

Luke left his dog, horses, and Bobby's at the livery stable, then made the short walk to the sheriff's office. He was about to open the door when he spotted a man across the street. He recognized him as one of the pair that had escaped the Rangers that morning. Luke turned, pulled his Colt, and leveled it at the man.

"Texas Ranger! You're under arrest. Don't even think of goin' for your gun."

The man raised his hands and smirked.

"I wouldn't dream of it, Ranger."

Luke felt the barrel of a gun shoved into the base of his spine.

"Drop the gun, Ranger," Sheriff Clayton ordered.

Luke complied. Clayton slugged him at the

base of his skull with the barrel of his pistol. Luke crumpled, stunned, still conscious, but unable to move.

"This is personal," Clayton muttered. He slid his revolver back in its holster.

"You're finally gonna come out in the open, brother," the outlaw said. "That's a real shame, because it's too late. I figure it had to be you who sicced the Rangers on us. That means I'm gonna kill you."

He grabbed for his gun, as did the sheriff. Both shot at almost the same moment. Clayton's brother went down, with a bullet in his belly. Clayton lowered his pistol, and crossed the street to where his brother had fallen.

"Damn you to Hell, Wilbur," his brother said, through clenched teeth. "I didn't think you had it in you to plug me. And I sure didn't figure you were faster on the draw."

"I just came to my senses, Wallace," the sheriff said. "However, it wasn't me who called in the Rangers. As far as beatin' you to the draw, I didn't."

He lowered the hand he had pressed to his stomach, revealing a bloody bullet hole. He coughed, gagged, then slumped across his brother's body.

15

Bobby regained consciousness a week later. As soon as Luke received word, he hurried over to check on his partner. He found Bobby sitting up in bed, with a clean white bandage tied around his chest. He was working on a bowl of chicken soup.

"Sure, I give you a job as a Ranger, and what do you go ahead and do? You sleep for a week, just when I needed you most."

"Luke! I'm so happy to see you," Bobby exclaimed. "How are you doin'? And what do you mean about needin' me?"

"I'm just about healed up," Luke answered. "I'd best catch you up on the news. After I left you here at the doc's, I headed over to the sheriff's office, to let him know what had happened. Who do I see across the street, but one of the hombres who got away from us."

"No! You're joshin' me."

"I am not. But here's where things got weird. When I went to arrest the bastard, the sheriff stuck a gun in my back. Then he bent his gun barrel over the back of my skull. Knocked me flat. Next thing I knew, the sheriff and that hombre drew on each other."

"Why? What happened?"

"They gut-shot each other. Clayton talked before he died. The other man was his brother, Wallace. They had an agreement. Wallace and his gang could do whatever they wanted, anywhere in Presidio County, as long as they stayed away from Alpine and Marfa. Wallace came lookin' for him after we hit their hideout. He figured his brother had called in the Rangers."

"I knew that sheriff was a liar," Bobby said. "What else?"

"The man who was with Wallace Clayton hung himself, after he found out the law would be closin' in on him. The barn was chock full of stolen goods. Apparently, the gang would smuggle them into Mexico. The Army turned up four more soldiers who were part of Clayton's bunch. They'll be court-martialed, and most likely hung."

"So that ends the gang," Bobby said.

"It does, but not our work," Luke answered. "There's plenty more muy malo hombres still runnin' loose. Our orders are to stay here, take over the county law until a new sheriff is appointed, and round up some more renegades. That is, if you ever get outta that bed. Oh, by the way, I have your first month's pay. I'll hold it for you, until you're up and around."

"You mean I get paid for havin' all this fun?"

"A whole thirty dollars a month, Bobby, just like I promised."

"Hey, how's my horse? How's Tony doin'?"

"That animal's as spoiled as mine. He's takin' things easy, along with Pete and RePete. Blaze has taken over one of the cells at the sheriff's office for his den. Listen, the doc told me I could only have a few minutes with you. I'll be back tomorrow. My best guess is we'll be here another two or three weeks, then head back to Austin. We'll stop in Junction on the way. I'll introduce you to my family. Just don't get too used to lyin' in bed. The Rangers'll never let you stay in one place for long."

"If the doc would let me, I'd be out of this bed right now," Bobby said.

"It'll be soon enough," Luke answered. "Hasta la vista, pardner."

"Hasta la vista, Lieutenant. And gracias."

About the Author

James J. Griffin, while a native New Englander, has been a lifelong horseman, and student of the Old West, particularly the Texas Rangers. He is considered an amateur historian of the Rangers, and has worked for many years in collaboration with the Texas Ranger Hall of Fame and Museum in Waco. He strives for historical accuracy in his writing, within the realm of fiction. Horses play a big part in Jim's stories, reflecting his love and knowledge of all things equine. He is a member of the Western Writers of America, Western Fictioneers, and a four time finalist for the Western Fictioneers Peacemaker Award. When not traveling out West, Jim makes his home in Keene, New Hampshire.

Center Point Large Print
600 Brooks Road / PO Box 1
Thorndike, ME 04986-0001 USA

(207) 568-3717

US & Canada:
1 800 929-9108
www.centerpointlargeprint.com